LET'S **HOP** TO IT!

WHAT **SURPRISES** AWAIT US?

NATIONAL
GEOGRAPHIC
KiDS

MORE
Surprising
Stories Behind
EVERYDAY
STUFF

STEPHANIE **WARREN DRIMMER**

NATIONAL GEOGRAPHIC
Washington, D.C.

TABLE OF **Contents**

Introduction 6

CHAPTER 1 •
Odds & Ends

CHAPTER 2 •
Playtime

CHAPTER 3 •
Wear It

CHAPTER 4 • Health
& Medicine

CHAPTER 5 •
Fabulous Food

Did you know that **haunted houses** were invited to keep teenagers out of **trouble?** That the **microwave** was invented by **accident?** Or that **wallpaper** once killed **people?**

HAVE YOU EVER THOUGHT

about where tape came from? What about
pizza, glue, or buttons? Sometimes it's the
most ordinary objects that are hiding the
most extraordinary stories.

Yo-yos were once decorated with jewels and
spun by nobles. The inventor of anesthesia
tested his creation by knocking himself
out. Meatballs didn't come from Italy.

Ready to be blown away by the things
you use every day? Turn the page!

CHAPTER 1

Odds & Ends

There's nothing very mysterious about adhesive tape and tissues ... or is there? Believe it or not, when you scribble with a pencil, patch a tear with tape—or even blow your nose!—you're using items with incredible backstories. Read on, and never look at your junk drawer the same way again.

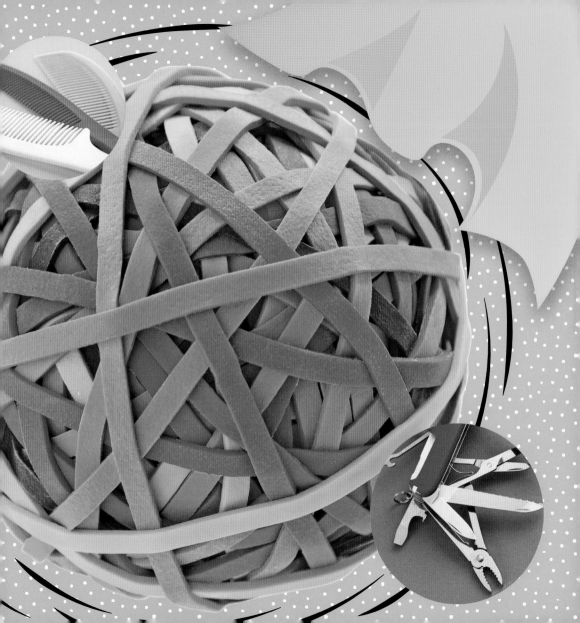

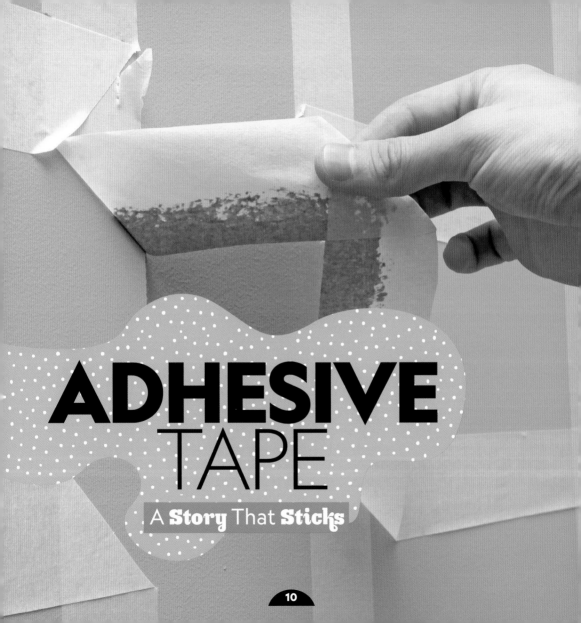

ADHESIVE
TAPE

A **Story** That **Sticks**

I'LL HELP YOU OUT OF A **STICKY** SITUATION.

Accidentally ripped your homework? Reach for the Scotch tape! Every household junk drawer seems to have a roll of the stuff—but how did this sticky fixer come to be?

Scotch tape was the brainchild of Richard Drew, a 23-year-old banjo player who boosted his income by delivering sandpaper samples for the manufacturing company 3M in Maplewood, Minnesota, U.S.A. One day in 1923, Drew dropped off a shipment to an auto shop, where he overheard workers complaining about the tough time they were having painting cars. To create a crisp paint line, they glued down paper—but when they removed the paper afterward, the glue often tore off the paint underneath. After two years of tinkering, Drew invented a sticky-but-not-too-sticky adhesive and applied it to strips of paper to create masking tape.

In 1929, Drew thought of a new use for his invention. At the time, fruit sellers were wrapping their produce with newly invented cellophane. But they needed an attractive way to seal the packaging. Drew coated some cellophane with his adhesive, creating the transparent version of the tape that we reach for today when working on that school project.

That same year, the Great Depression threw America into the worst financial crisis of modern world history. People were looking for new ways to be thrifty, and Scotch tape could help them extend the lives of everyday items, from repairing torn clothing, mending paper products, and even sealing up cracked eggs! It's stuck around ever since.

Bet You **Didn't Know**

People had a hard time finding the start of the roll until the tape dispenser came along in 1932.

PENCIL

A Sharp Idea

One day long ago, a Stone Age person reached into the ashes of an old fire, pulled out a piece of charcoal, and used it to scribble on a piece of stone. It was the world's first writing implement.

Charcoal is a version of the element carbon, and modern pencils are still made of the stuff—but in a slightly different form called graphite. Naturally soft, graphite is an ideal writing material because it marks things easily. In 1564, England got a massive source of it when— according to legend—a severe storm uprooted a large oak tree in the county of Cumbria, revealing a treasure trove underneath: a huge deposit of graphite in the ground.

The first pencils were made by cutting graphite into thin rods, then wrapping them in string or sandwiching them between pieces of wood. Because of its graphite deposit, England had a hold on

THE PENCIL IS MIGHTIER THAN THE CLUB!

the pencil market. So when the English cut off their supply of graphite to France during the French Revolution, the French had to get creative.

Enter Nicolas-Jacques Conté, a one-eyed inventor who once made hot-air balloons for Napoleon's army. In 1795, he mixed diluted graphite dust with clay, then baked it until it hardened. He'd invented a way to make usable graphite from inferior sources. That meant pencils could be mass-produced all around the world. Write on!

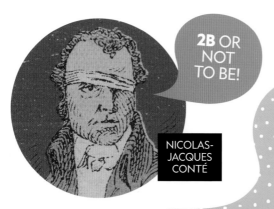

2B OR NOT TO BE!

NICOLAS-JACQUES CONTÉ

Bet You **Didn't Know**

Despite the common nickname, there is no lead in pencils. The case of mistaken identity occurred because graphite looks a lot like lead.

SWISS ARMY
KNIFE

Folding Phenom

GET THAT AWAY FROM ME!

Soldiers on a battlefield might need to cut through undergrowth, repair their weapons, and open a can of food—but they can't be weighed down by heavy tools. Solution: the Swiss Army knife.

The soldiers of the Swiss Army were not the first to wield a multipurpose tool—not by a long shot. Dating back 1,800 years, Roman soldiers used a tool that included a knife, a fork, a spoon, a pick, and a spike—possibly for eating snails, a popular food at the time.

The modern Swiss Army knife got its start in 1886, when all Swiss troops were issued a folding pocketknife with a wooden handle. A few years later, soldiers began using a new kind of rifle that could be taken apart for cleaning with a screwdriver. Rather than asking soldiers to carry a separate tool, engineers added a screwdriver to their knife, along with an awl (a tool for making holes), and a can opener for good measure.

In 1891, Swiss silverware manufacturer Karl Elsener began producing a line of multi-purpose tools. He made different versions for different people, from the Student, which came in a small size, to the Farmer, which included a wood saw. Today, the company produces about 28,000 Swiss Army knives every day. Some models include attachments such as USB drives, MP3 players, and even a tool for performing emergency surgeries. That's one nifty knife!

ONE GIANT LEAP FOR KNIFE-KIND!

Bet You **Didn't Know**

No NASA mission since the 1970s has left Earth without a Swiss Army knife on board.

KID Geniuses!

Inventors don't always bustle around laboratories, peering into beakers and adjusting Bunsen burners. Many inventions were thought up by regular people who simply saw a smart solution to a problem. Some were even kids—just like you!

Toy Trucks

In 1962, five-year-old Robert Patch used some spare shoeboxes, bottle caps, and nails to come up with a new kind of toy. He invented a truck that could be converted from a van to a dump truck and back again. Patch's father thought the idea had potential, and he helped his son apply for a patent. Only six years old at the time, Patch signed his name with an X—but he became the youngest person to ever receive a U.S. patent!

Popsicle

In 1905, an 11-year-old kid named Frank Epperson from San Francisco, California, U.S.A., mixed up a concoction of sugary powder and water, then left it outside for the night with the stirring stick still inside the container. In the morning, his experiment had frozen into an icy treat. Years later, Epperson patented his invention under the name "Epsicle," after himself—but his children came up with a better name: Popsicle.

Crayon Holder

When crayons break or get worn down into tiny stubs, they can be too small to hold on to. In 1999, 11-year-old Cassidy Goldstein came up with an ingenious solution to this problem: She stuck her crayon nubs into clear plastic tubes designed to hold flowers, making them easier to grip. Goldstein patented her idea in 2002, and sales of her Crayon Holders helped her pay for college.

Snowmobile

Fourteen-year-old Joseph-Armand Bombardier, who grew up in Quebec, Canada, in the 1920s, had a habit of taking apart everything around the house. So to keep his son busy, Bombardier's father bought him a broken Ford Model T engine. After more than a year of tinkering, Bombardier had repaired his old engine, mounted it on wooden skis, and attached an airplane propeller on the back. The snowmobile was born!

Trampoline

In 1930, the traveling circus came to Cedar Rapids, Iowa, U.S.A., entrancing a local kid named George Nissen. As the 16-year-old watched trapeze artists finish their routines by dropping into a safety net, he wondered: What if they could fall into something that would bounce them even higher? With the help of his high school gymnastics coach, Nissen used scrap steel, tire tubes, and canvas material to build the first trampoline in his garage.

TOGETHER WE SHALL REACH **NEW HEIGHTS!**

RUBBER BAND

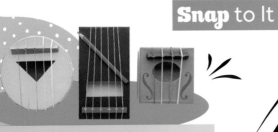

From holding a stack of papers together to sealing up an open bag to crafting a DIY stringed instrument, there are tons of practical and creative uses for rubber bands. But how did this simple yet extremely useful object come to be?

Before the rubber band could be invented, rubber had to be invented. The Aztec and the Maya were making this flexible material an astounding 3,000 years ago. They would drain the milky-colored sap from native *Hevea brasiliensis* trees—later called rubber trees—and mix it with liquid squeezed from morning glory vines. The combination hardened into a

RUBBER TREE
SAP BEING
COLLECTED

Bet You **Didn't Know**

More than 14 million
pounds (6.4 million kg)
of rubber bands are
made each year.

sturdy substance that they used to make all kinds of things, including sandals and balls.

Spanish explorers encountered this material when they arrived in South America in the 16th century. But rubber didn't get its modern name until 1770, when British chemist Joseph Priestley noticed that if he rubbed it on paper, it removed pencil marks. That discovery gave the substance its new name: rubber—and at the same time, invented the eraser. It was the first of many products made of rubber.

In 1819, Englishman Thomas Hancock was manufacturing rubber suspenders, gloves, shoes, and socks designed to keep people dry while traveling via stagecoach. To use up the leftovers, he invented a machine that formed the rubber scraps into small bands. But if they were exposed to cold temperatures, the bands became brittle and snapped. It wasn't until 1833 that Charles Goodyear invented a process of heating rubber to a high temperature and adding sulfur to make it tougher, called vulcanization (page 75). Suddenly stretchy *and* strong, rubber bands sprang into service worldwide.

MASON JAR

A **Can-Do** Design

Mason jars are trendy. You can spot them filled with gourmet ingredients on restaurant shelves and even serving as candle holders and vases at weddings. But they got their start as a solution to an age-old problem: how to save food for the future without it going rotten.

The issue of food spoilage got real during Napoleon's conquest of Europe in the early 19th century, when soldiers would trek long distances only to discover their rations had rotted. Napoleon offered a prize of 12,000 French francs—a high sum at the time—to anyone who came up with a good method of preserving food. The prizewinner was a candymaker named Nicolas Appert, who invented the process of canning: sealing food in jars heated to a high temperature to kill off any wiggling microbes.

By 1803, the French army was eating food out of jars sealed with Appert's method. But his cork-and-wax apparatus was tricky to

use. Often, the seal didn't work properly, and soldiers would open a jar to find that their goods had gone bad. That all changed in 1858, when John Landis Mason introduced a design with a screw-on lid that created an airtight seal, and a clear glass container that meant people could easily see the contents of the jar. The Mason jar—named after its inventor—revolutionized food storage for soldiers and citizens alike. They're still holding our drinks, jams, and leftovers today.

I'VE GOT A **JARRING IDEA.**

JOHN LANDIS MASON

Bet You **Didn't Know**

Before Mason jars, canning containers were opaque, meaning not see-through, preventing anyone from seeing what was inside. Talk about a mystery meal!

COMBS

A **Knotty** Problem

MY LUSCIOUS LOCKS!

You know a comb is good for getting the knots out of unruly hair. But did you know that a few thousand years ago, it had a different—and some might say disgusting—function?

The earliest known combs date back some 6,000 years and were made of dried-out fish skeletons. Later versions were made with other types of animal bone and ivory. One comb decorated with a hippo was found in an ancient Egyptian tomb dating back to 3500 B.C.—even before the pharaohs ruled!

In 1989, two scientists were examining a first-century hair comb dug out of the ground in the West Bank near Israel when they saw something they weren't expecting. Lodged between the comb's teeth were 10 long-dead head lice and 27 louse eggs. The ancient comb wasn't used for detangling—instead, it was for removing the pesky parasites!

LOUSE

Perhaps the discovery shouldn't have been so surprising—lice were a fact of life and people combed them out of their hair as part of their everyday routine. In the Middle Ages, combs were engraved with intricate carvings, including scenes from the Bible. People even gave combs inscribed with French phrases like *pour bien* ("for your comfort") as a token of love. Eww la la!

Bet You **Didn't Know**

The average hairbrush has almost 3,500 colonies of bacteria on every square inch (6.5 sq cm).

ALL **Natural**

Not all useful tools had to be invented. Many of our handiest materials were already out there in nature, just waiting to be discovered.

Loofah

Some people think old-fashioned loofahs are sea sponges. While that's not true, they do come from nature—loofahs are actually a type of gourd, or hard-skinned fruit similar to a pumpkin. Once cleaned and dried, they make the perfect shower scrubber. People have been cultivating loofahs for so long experts aren't sure where they originated, but until the late 19th century in the United States, when baths became popular, they were usually used to scrub teapots. Today, most loofahs are made with synthetic materials.

Pumice

Modern people use these rough stones to rub calluses off their feet. But the ancients found many more uses for pumice, a stone that forms when superheated lava spews from an erupting volcano and then cools down quickly. Romans used it to rub off unwanted body hair and mixed it with lime (a powdery substance) to make plaster for building. Egyptians mixed it with vinegar and brushed their teeth with it.

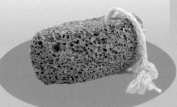

Shellac

You might not have heard of this substance, but it's the stuff that makes all kinds of wood furniture, such as tables and chairs, shiny. And this smooth glaze comes from a surprising source: a bug! Lac bugs gather in huge groups on trees in Thailand and India, where the females secrete resin onto the tree bark. For at least 3,000 years, humans have been scraping off that resin and using it to set jewels in sword hilts, paint palaces, and finish furniture.

Silk

Did you know that soft, luxurious silk comes from worms? It only takes two or three days for a three-inch (8-cm)-long silkworm to spin about a mile (1.6 km) of thin, delicate silk strand. Silkworms use the stuff to weave their cocoons, but starting around 3000 B.C., the people of China learned it also made excellent thread. Silk became a luxury material coveted worldwide.

Pearls

These milky white orbs come to be when a tiny bit of grit finds its way inside an oyster shell. To protect itself from the irritating intruder, the oyster covers it with layers of nacre, the substance that also makes up its shell. In the ancient past, divers had to hold their breath and descend 100 feet (30 m) in the hopes of finding an oyster with a pearl inside. Today, many pearls are cultivated by farmers who slip grit inside oyster shells, then wait.

TISSUES

Nothing to **Sneeze** At

Ahh-ahh-ACHOO! When you feel a sneeze coming on, you reach for the nearest box of tissues. But their original purpose was not to blot snot; it was to bandage wounds.

During World War I, a cotton shortage meant the U.S. Army desperately needed a replacement material for binding up war injuries. A small U.S. company called Kimberly-Clark stepped into service with cellucotton, an artificial fabric made of wood fiber. Five times more absorbent than cotton and half the price to manufacture, it was immediately pressed into service for surgical bandages and air filters on gas masks.

When the war ended, Kimberly-Clark was left holding a huge surplus of the material. Instead of throwing in the artificial towel,

the company heads got creative. They came up with a new peacetime product: a disposable cloth that women could use to remove their makeup. Soon ladies complained about their husbands commandeering the cloths to blow their noses instead.

In 1921, Kimberly-Clark started selling cellucotton sheets in a pop-up tissue box. For the first time, people had a convenient way to deal with an unexpected sneeze. The company still hoped to find other uses for its product, though. They tried marketing tissues as furniture dusters, windshield cleaners, and even the ideal thing to blot grease from french fries. But the people had spoken: The cellucotton creation was destined to be used to catch sneezes.

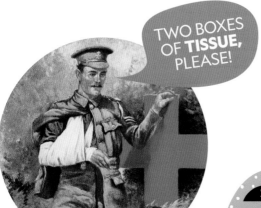

TWO BOXES OF **TISSUE,** PLEASE!

GLUE
Amazing Adhesive

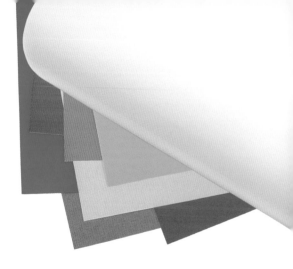

Today, we use glue for everything from art projects to manufacturing cars. Humans have, in fact, been sticking one thing to another (and probably accidentally gluing their fingers together) for a very long time.

In an ancient South African cave, archaeologists discovered Paleolithic stone tools bearing traces of a dark, sticky substance dating back 70,000 years. That substance was bitumen, a naturally occurring material now used for surfacing roads and waterproofing roofs. Back then, our ancestors were using it to affix wooden handles to stone blades, creating tools that made daily tasks like chopping up meat a bit easier.

Early humans experimented with all kinds of materials to make glue. They boiled the hides, horns, bones, hooves, and some tissue of animals to produce one type of adhesive, and they used the skin and bones of fish to make another. These early glues helped in the making of pottery, utensils, and weapons.

Modern scientists are still experimenting to try to come up with stickier and stronger glues. In 1951, American scientists were running tests on a substance called ethyl cyanoacrylate when they became curious to find out how the stuff bent light. They applied it to a piece of expensive lab equipment—where it promptly stuck! The new substance became known as superglue. Today, scientists are looking to animals with amazing sticking powers—like barnacles that cling to the sides of boats and geckos that can stick upside down to ceilings—to discover the next great glue.

Bet You **Didn't Know**

Victorian women
used an early
type of glue as
hair gel.

29

INDEX CARDS

A **Noteworthy** Idea

These simple paper rectangles were invented with a lofty goal in mind—to organize every known animal, plant, and mineral in the world.

Index cards were the brainchild of one of science's greatest heroes: Carl Linnaeus. Before the Swedish botanist and physician came along, there was no system for classifying organisms. Scientists named species willy-nilly: a tomato, for example, was called *Solanum caule inermi herbaceo, foliis pinnatis incisis.* Try memorizing that!

Linnaeus thought there had to be a better way. He wanted to organize life-forms based on how they were related to one another, a branch of science now called taxonomy. He started with plants he collected in the woods near his home. Before long, scientists were sending him specimens from as far away as China and Africa. Soon, Linnaeus had more than 12,000 species to classify. Around 1765,

he hit on the perfect system: writing their names on small pieces of sturdy paper, three inches by five inches (7.6 by 12.7 cm) in size, that could be grouped, moved, and reshuffled until every creature had a category.

It was such a brilliant idea that all kinds of people with information in need of organizing adopted it. Librarians, for example, used the system for cataloging their books from 1791 until the 21st century (when computers took over). Today, they're still going strong as flash cards.

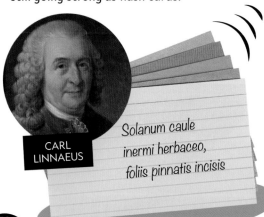

CARL LINNAEUS

Solanum caule inermi herbaceo, foliis pinnatis incisis

Apple Crisp
4 cups sliced apples
2/3 cups brown sugar
1 cup plain flour

Bet You **Didn't Know**

In 1895, Brussels, Belgium, housed the world's first search engine: the Mundaneum, a catalog of more than 12 million index cards meant to contain all the world's knowledge. Curious people could write in with a question, and workers would send them a list of books and articles with the answer in return.

CHAPTER 2

Playtime

Prehistoric kids loved to play just as much as modern ones: They had yo-yos, dolls, and even kid-size toy chariots! Modern kids fling Skee-Balls and squish slime—but these toys are much more than just for fun. Read on to learn the puzzling past of some everyday playthings.

SILLY **PUTTY**

It's squishy, it's stretchy, it's bouncy. This strange substance has been entertaining kids for more than 70 years. But Silly Putty wasn't even meant to be a toy.

When World War II began, rubber became one of the most important resources to the war effort: It was essential for military tools, such as tires, boots, gas masks, and life rafts. U.S. civilians were asked to donate all kinds of rubber goods, but a shortage loomed. So the American government tasked U.S. company General Electric with coming up with a substitute substance.

Engineer James Wright started tinkering in his lab. When he mixed boric acid and silicone oil, he created a gob of goo with fascinating properties: It was really bouncy, super stretchy, and would not decay or melt. It was not quite right for making tires and boots, so the U.S. government wasn't interested. But Wright thought it must be good for something. He sent samples of his "nutty putty" around the world, hoping somebody would come up with a use for his invention.

One of those samples bounced its way into a party, where it caught the attention of a businessman named Peter Hodgson. Noticing that the guests couldn't stop playing with the stuff, he realized it would make a great toy. He renamed it "Silly Putty," packaged it in plastic eggs, and started selling it around Easter time. Silly Putty went on to become one of history's top-selling toys, with more than 300 million eggs produced since 1950. That's a lot of goo!

PUTTY **GOING** PLACES!

Bet You **Didn't Know**

In 1968, Apollo 8 astronauts took Silly Putty into orbit with them to stick down their tools in zero gravity.

BICYCLES

A **Wheel-y Cool** Invention

OUT OF MY WAY, BOYS!

If you could travel back in time to take a ride on the world's first bicycle, you might be confused: It had no pedals!

That version, which riders had to power by "walking" along with their feet, was the brainchild of German engineer Baron Karl Drais von Sauerbronn, who invented the machine to help him coast around the parks of Paris. It never caught on, but it did inspire other inventors to come up with a better model. The first modern-style pedal bike rolled up in 1867. But its wooden wheels made for a very bumpy ride, giving it a nickname—the "boneshaker"—that wasn't exactly good for sales.

The first bicycle to become really popular wasn't much better. The British penny-farthing had a giant front wheel and a tiny back one (it was named for the smallest and largest coins at the time). The design meant riders sat dangerously high off the ground. Despite all kinds of accidents, Victorian people became obsessed with these odd-wheeled vehicles because

ORVILLE WRIGHT

Bet You **Didn't Know**

Orville and Wilbur Wright built the first flying airplane in a bicycle repair shop in Dayton, Ohio, U.S.A.

BMX BIKE

they were a novel way to escape the grimy city and visit the countryside.

In the 1880s, less hazardous versions of the penny-farthing called "safety bicycles" were wheeled out. They had pedals attached to gears, a chain that moved the rear wheel, and shock absorbers. The modern bicycle took off.

SKEE-BALL

Arcade Amusement

Send a ball rolling down a knee-high ramp, hopping over a bump, and flying—hopefully—into a hole marked with a number. Rack up enough points, and you can win a plastic toy or a small stuffed animal. It's Skee-Ball, a fixture of nearly every arcade. How did it get there?

In the early 1900s, Joseph Fourestier Simpson wanted nothing more than to leave a lasting legacy. He was always dreaming up new products, such as an egg crate that prevented shells from cracking during transport. But his biggest hit turned out to be a game: Participants lobbed a ball up a ramp and over a hump, trying to land it in a hole for points. Simpson called it Skee-Ball, a play on ski jumping.

One fan of the game, J. Dickinson Este, thought Skee-Ball had the potential to be an arcade hit. But first, he shortened the game's original 36-foot (11-m) lane to the modern 10-foot (3-m) length. Then he threw everything he had into marketing Skee-Ball, installing machines on boardwalks, at colleges, and even in New York City's Times Square.

It worked. The advertising got the game noticed, and the size change made it more arcade-friendly. It also meant that kids—who hadn't been strong enough to roll the ball 36 feet—could participate. The game remains basically unchanged today.

Bet You **Didn't Know**

Around 1916, Skee-Ball was considered a vice, and it was banned on Sundays in some cities.

Dolls AROUND THE WORLD

What do you picture when you think of a doll? You might think of a baby look-alike with wide eyes and rosy cheeks. Or maybe a doll carved from wood. Or decorated with beads. Or even stacked one inside another. It all depends on where you're from in the world!

Kokeshi: Japan

Originating in the Tohoku region of northern Japan, these handmade wooden dolls date back to the early 19th century. Woodworkers at the time started carving simple, limbless figures to sell to tourists. Dollmakers use intricate painted patterns, passed down through generations, for decoration.

I LITERALLY CONTAIN MULTITUDES!

Matryoshka: Russia

Open a Matryoshka doll and you might be surprised to find that there's another doll inside, and another and another! The nesting dolls symbolize family and get their name from a traditional Russian girls' name, Matrona, which comes from the Latin word for "mother." The largest set of Matryoshka dolls ever made had 51 figures stacked inside!

Ndebele Doll: South Africa

The Ndebele women of South Africa traditionally adorn themselves with bright capes, beaded hoops around their necks and ankles, and clothing with colorful, geometric patterns. And they're known for their miniature dolls dressed in the same style. In the past, Ndebele dolls were made in secret by a grandmother and given to a new bride on her wedding day.

Alebrijes: Mexico

In Mexico, dolls don't always look like miniature people. Alebrijes are imaginary creatures that combine features of different animals, such as the wings of a bat, the teeth of a wolf, and the body of a dog. They were first made in the 1930s by a man named Pedro Linares Lopez, an expert maker of piñatas who switched to creating fantastical paper alebrijes.

BATS AND **WOLVES** AND **DOGS,** OH MY!

Worry Dolls: Guatemala

These tiny dolls made of sticks, wire, thread, and scrap fabrics are traditionally made by the indigenous highland people of Guatemala. According to legend, if your worries are keeping you up at night, you simply tell them to your dolls—one worry doll for each trouble—and then place them under your pillow. When you wake up, your worries will be gone.

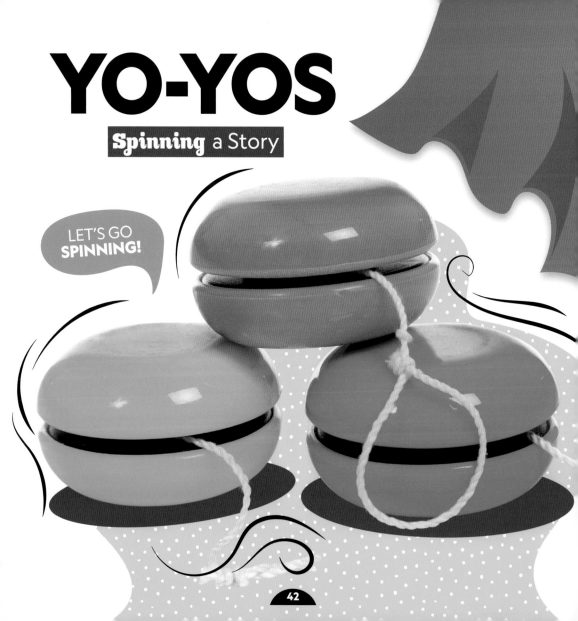

According to a popular myth, the yo-yo didn't start out as a toy, but as a weapon. As the story goes, hunters in the Philippines used to hurl a lethal version made of large wood disks and heavy twine, ensnaring animals' legs in its ropes. But it remains unclear if this tale is more fantasy than folklore.

The yo-yo is one ancient toy: A Greek vase more than 1,500 years old shows a boy playing with a spinning disk! The idea proved so popular that it spread across the world: By the late 1700s, fashionable European nobles were spinning yo-yos decorated with jewels and painted with intricate shapes that blurred into patterns when in motion.

Yo-yos didn't reach the United States until the 1920s, when a Filipino immigrant named Pedro Flores started playing with the toy on one of his breaks from his job as a bellhop at a California hotel. Seeing

a business opportunity, Flores started manufacturing the toy himself. His version was different from earlier ones: It had a string that was looped around the axle instead of tied to it.

For the first time, the new design made it possible for yo-yo aficionados to perform all kinds of tricks, from "Around the World" to "Walk the Dog." Today, there's a World Yo-Yo Contest every year, featuring players from more than 30 countries competing to show off their spinning skills!

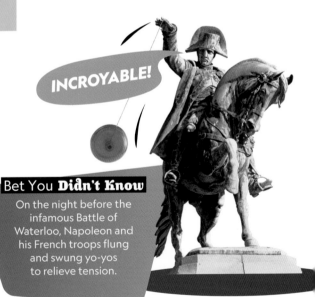

INCROYABLE!

Bet You **Didn't Know**

On the night before the infamous Battle of Waterloo, Napoleon and his French troops flung and swung yo-yos to relieve tension.

DOLLHOUSES

Mini **Mansions**

Their miniature rooms are filled with teensy tables, little lamps, and puny paintings. They're one of the most classic kids' toys around. But did you know that dollhouses weren't originally meant for play at all?

The first dollhouses appeared in the 17th century, mainly in Germany, Holland, and England. Called a *dockenhaus* (German for "small house") or "cabinet house," the fronts opened on hinges to reveal the objects inside. At the time, collecting expensive miniature objects was a cool adult hobby, and people used dollhouses to show off their tiny treasures.

Soon after, mini metal houses that might contain details like teeny fireplaces, pots, and straw brooms became popular in Germany. But they weren't toys: Mothers used the tiny houses as models to teach their daughters about cleaning, cooking, and organizing. In the 18th century, the "Baby House" was a big hit in England.

Bet You **Didn't Know**

The YouTube channel Tiny Kitchen features meals made in a working miniature kitchen. Everything is about the size of a pinkie fingernail, whether it's a stack of pancakes or a chili cheese dog.

WELCOME
TO MY
DOCKENHAUS!

This tiny home was an exact model of the owner's actual house, with everything from drapes to door-knobs perfectly copied.

It wasn't until the industrial revolution, beginning in the 18th century, that factory manufacturing made it possible to mass-produce objects—including miniature ones. That development took the dollhouse from a luxury good to a kids' toy. Recently, dollhouses have become trendy again, with artisans selling tiny toilets and itty-bitty blankets online. There are even social media sites that showcase all things minuscule, from toasters to milk bottles.

45

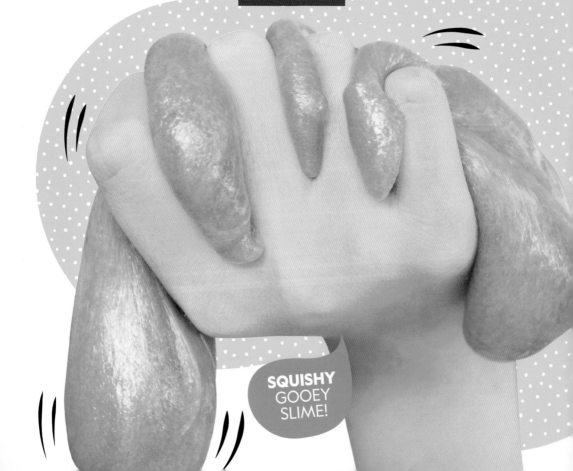

SLIME

Great **Goo**

SQUISHY GOOEY SLIME!

It's ooey. It's sticky and slick and gross. It's also fun. It's slime! It might seem like this glop was glopped on planet Earth from outer space. But what's the real story?

Slime first splatted onto the scene on the kids' TV network Nickelodeon. In 1981, the channel aired a Canadian sketch comedy show called *You Can't Do That on Television.* Every time one of the actors on the show said "I don't know," a bucket of green slime drenched them.

Kids loved the slimings so much that Nickelodeon started making them a feature on other shows. On the 1986 trivia game show *Double Dare,* contestants who didn't know the answer to a question could opt to compete in a "physical challenge" that often ended with them being drenched in slime.

Soon, slime had dribbled its way onto toy store shelves. The packaged version was

WHO NEEDS **KETCHUP?**

JUSTIN BIEBER

made of guar gum—a thickening agent that's an ingredient in many packaged foods—and sodium borate, which binds the substance together. Soon, there were slime Popsicles and even a Green Slime Geyser, unveiled in 1990 at Universal Studios theme park in Florida, U.S.A. Today, many science books take slime to the next squishy step, teaching kids how to make their own at home.

Ancient TOYS

Kids of the past may not have had video games or remote-controlled race cars. But they played with toys just like children of today. Some of these play-things might look unfamiliar—but others are surprisingly similar to modern toys!

Roman Doll

This doll was discovered in the elaborate marble tomb of an eight-year-old girl who likely lived in the second century A.D. Objects like this doll were long thought to be offerings to the gods, but experts now think many were actually toys.

European Knight

This figure of a knight mounted atop his trusty steed is one of the earliest surviving toy soldiers. It was made in the 13th or 14th century A.D. and cast in bronze. Experts think many of these toys were probably made, but few survive today— maybe because ancient kids were rough with them!

THEY CALL HIM **SIR WINS-A-LOT!**

Turkish Chariot

Kids today often drive around in child-size toy cars—so it makes sense that children of the past would have done the same with chariots! Archaeologists discovered a 5,000-year-old child-size clay chariot during a dig in the ancient city of Sogmatar, Turkey.

Greek Horse

In school, ancient Greek kids studied subjects like math, literature, and science. (Only boys went to school, except in the city-state of Sparta, where girls were trained to be warriors.) When they weren't hitting the books, kids kept busy with games like hide-and-seek and toys such as this wooden horse on wheels that dates back to around 900 B.C.

Mesopotamian Game

Known as the Royal Game of Ur, this ancient board game was discovered in Mesopotamia (modern-day Iraq) and is at least 4,400 years old. People of all ages and social classes played board games—several were even found in the tomb of the Egyptian pharaoh Tutankhamun.

African Game

This is one ancient game you might have played yourself. Mancala is one of the oldest games in the world and has been part of leisure time in countries across Africa since about A.D. 600. Although people of the past might have used small stones or seeds as playing pieces, the board game has remained essentially unchanged.

RATTLE

Shake It Up

Humans have been shaking rattles for thousands and thousands of years. But the earliest ones weren't used for play: Instead, ancient people believed that the noisemakers could frighten away evil spirits. People shook rattles during births, sicknesses, and deaths—or whenever they thought ghouls and ghosts were walking the Earth. Often, these rattles were made of shells, rawhide, or leather, with corn, rocks, beans, or seeds inside to make the noise.

In 2015, archaeologists unearthed eight small figurines made of horn in the shapes of animals like birds, elk, and boars near Lake Itkul in Russia. At 4,500 years old, they were truly ancient. Since the figures were hollow inside, experts suspect that long ago they might have been rattles used to entertain prehistoric infants.

Around 1360 B.C., Egyptian children played with rattles shaped like birds, pigs, and bears. Made of clay and covered in silk, they were carefully

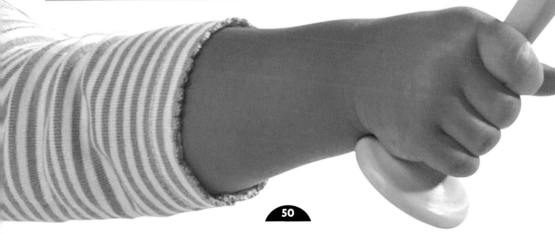

BEWARE, **GHOULIES!**

designed without any sharp points that could harm infants: Pigs' ears were small and rounded, for example, and birds didn't have feet or pointy beaks.

But rattles made of clay could break easily, making them unsafe for a baby. By the 1800s, silversmiths were casting silver rattles that infants could chew on without injuring themselves. The idea stayed popular among well-to-do families: In the early 20th century, silver rattles made by New York jeweler Tiffany & Co. were considered the ultimate luxury baby gift.

I HAD THOSE BRITS **RATTLED!**

AFRICAN GOURD RATTLE

Bet You **Didn't Know**

One American rattle-making silversmith was Paul Revere, better known for his midnight ride in 1775 to alert the colonists that the British army was approaching.

What's a nine-letter word for a very popular letter game? If you said "crossword," you might have a knack for this classic word puzzle.

Though the idea behind the game is incredibly simple, crosswords were only invented about a century ago. A journalist named Arthur Wynne created the first one in response to a challenge to think up a new printed game for the New York newspaper he worked for. Though it was shaped like a diamond and had no blacked-out squares, Wynne's crossword looked very similar to those of today. It appeared in the December 21, 1913, issue of the paper and proved to be a smashing success.

Within months, Wynne's puzzle was picked up by other newspapers and reprinted all over the country. By the early 1920s, the public had gone crossword-crazy; every major U.S. newspaper had its own. In 1924, crossword puzzle books became four of the top best sellers of the day. A few years later, crosswords were being printed in almost every language.

The fad continued, and by the early 1930s, crosswords were being printed on dresses, shoes, handbags, and jewelry. Today, there are about 200,000 subscribers to the crossword puzzle service of the *New York Times*—maker of the world's most famous puzzle. The question is, how many of those subscribers are solving Monday's easier puzzles, and how many conquer Saturday's arduous (a seven-letter word for "difficult") crosswords?

Bet You **Didn't Know**

Anyone can submit a crossword to the *New York Times* for publication. The youngest person to successfully construct one was 13 years old!

PIGGY BANK

The Whole **Hog**

Do you save your pennies and allowance in a special container? Though today they're shaped like everything from airplanes to elephants, these containers are traditionally called "piggy banks." But why would a pig be the perfect place to store money?

Today, most people use banks to keep their money secure. Where did people store their cash before banks existed? During the Middle Ages, many hid their money in kitchen jars, hoping burglars would be less likely to spot cash between the pickles and jams. But they didn't use jars made of glass or metal, which were too expensive for the average person. Instead, most kitchenware was made of a kind of orange clay called pygg. So people called their money jars pygg banks.

SAVING IS COOL!

54

I'M **BROKE!**

Bet You **Didn't Know**

Early piggy banks had no hole in the bottom, so they had to be smashed to get the money out.

Over time, the early English word for pig, *picga*, evolved into "pigge." By the 19th century, the words for the "pigge" animal and the "pygg" clay were pronounced the same—so potters began to make pygg banks in the shape of the barnyard beast.

Today, piggy banks are a symbol of financial know-how. In some European countries, pigs are associated with good fortune, so it's customary to give piggy banks as gifts.

CHAPTER 3

Wear It

It might not seem like it, but when you zip up your hoodie or put on a baseball cap, you become part of a history that stretches way back in time—we're talking up to thousands of years! Clothing is more than a way to keep people warm and covered up; it also lets them make a statement. These stories will make you see your closet in a whole new light.

BUTTONS

Fascinating **Fastener**

Just as you're getting to the last button on your shirt, you hear the *plink* of something falling to the floor and rolling away. Oh no! You lost a button.

I BET THE ZIPPER COULDN'T PAY YOUR BILLS!

Today we think of buttons as functional, there to keep our clothes firmly around our bodies. But for most of the button's history, it was just for looks! The earliest known buttons, made of shell and dating back to about 2000 B.C., were found in the Indus Valley in what is now Pakistan. But they had no buttonholes to go with them—that idea would take another 3,000 years.

Before the buttonhole was invented, clothing had to be flowy enough to wiggle into, or else it had to be draped around the body and fastened in place with brooches, buckles, or pins. But when buttons became functional in about the 13th century, they allowed clothing designs to be slimmer and more close-fitting.

People went button-crazy. By the medieval period, buttons were a status symbol for showing off how wealthy you were. Some people wore such valuable buttons that they could be used for paying debts—pluck off one or two and the bill was settled. The more buttons on your outfit, the more important you were. To this day, Italians refer to the places where powerful leaders meet as *stanze dei bottoni*, or "rooms of the buttons."

I WEAR MY HEART ON **MY SLEEVE!**

Bet You **Didn't Know**

From the 13th to the 15th centuries, buttons were often used to fasten detachable sleeves onto women's clothing. Ladies swapped their sleeves between outfits and even gave them to suitors as love tokens.

DIAPER

Waste **Management**

Babies have big round eyes, toothless smiles, and adorably pudgy bodies. But before they're toilet-trained, some might say infants are also an accident waiting to happen!

Parents in different regions have used different methods to contain the mess. The Chukchi, the indigenous people of frigid northeastern Siberia, simply put their babies in fur bags filled with dried moss to absorb moisture. In medieval Europe, parents wound strips of cloth called swaddling around and around the baby. The process was so tiresome that parents wouldn't change the material for at least three days. Imagine the odor!

People started looking for a better solution when the industrial revolution began in the 18th century. For the first time, working-class people were earning enough money to buy beautiful furniture, and they didn't want their infants soiling their sofas. The 1849 invention of the safety pin made it easier to keep crude cloth diapers from sliding off. But washing and drying diapers was a big job, and when women joined the

POOP! THERE IT IS!

workforce during World War II, they no longer had the time. Many relied on laundry services, which would deliver clean diapers and pick up dirty ones once a week.

The next big diaper change came in the 1940s with the arrival of a disposable version. New and better models have been appearing ever since, from super-absorbent materials to elasticized holes for the baby's legs—to keep infants (and sofas!) clean and dry.

Bet You **Didn't Know**

The average American baby goes through 8,000 diapers.

I COME BEARING **GIFTS!**

PURSE

History in the Bag

I GO PLACES!

Before the Middle Ages, if you wanted to carry your valuables around with you, you would wrap them up in a piece of fabric and hide the bundle in a fold of your clothing. This might have kept your belongings safe from thieves, but it was cumbersome—and not exactly comfortable.

By the early 13th century, the bundle had evolved into a sack often made of leather and worn by both men and women, usually attached to a belt. At first this bag was called a *bursa,* Latin for "hide," but over time, that morphed into "purse." A thief who sliced an unsuspecting victim's purse straps and grabbed the goods was called a "cutpurse"—a word still in use today.

Bet You **Didn't Know**

In 2016, a diamond-encrusted handbag sold at auction for $300,168.

I AM JUST **MURSE- UNDERSTOOD!**

Purses for men went out of style around the end of the 16th century, when pockets became commonplace. Fashionable ladies of the time used their purses as status symbols. They displayed them on a *chatelaine,* a hook attached to a belt and festooned with chains for attaching small household items, such as keys, scissors, and knife cases. Women of high status wore chatelaines made out of precious metals to show off their wealth.

In the 17th and 18th centuries, purses briefly went out of fashion as women switched to pockets, which they concealed inside their voluminous skirts. But when straight, sleek dresses with no room for pockets came into vogue in the early 1900s, women began carrying the first modern-style purses, often slung over their shoulders on a cord or chain. They haven't put them down since.

CARDIGAN

Buttoned **Up**

The cardigan isn't exactly thought of as a high-fashion item—most of us don't give this closet staple much consideration. But this mild-mannered sweater got its start in an unexpected place: on the battlefield.

Cardigans are named after their inventor: James Thomas Brudenell, the seventh Earl of Cardigan. The earl was a lieutenant general in the British army in the 19th century, and he was known for his lavish style: He spent extravagantly every year on well-made new uniforms for his soldiers. His major claim to fame came during the Crimean War. On October 25, 1854, the earl—wearing a collarless knitted coat—led a cavalry regiment against Russian forces. This Charge of the Light Brigade became so famous it was immortalized in a poem by Alfred Lord Tennyson.

The real event wasn't nearly as grand as its reputation: The truth is, the earl chickened out at the last minute and turned tail for home! He was hailed as a hero when he got to London (before the truth came out), and knitted jackets like the one he wore became the must-have piece of the day.

The earl's cowardice was eventually revealed, but by then the British had grown to so love the cozy coats named in his honor that they kept on wearing them. Soon after, in 1883, the cardigan earned a permanent place in the closet when French designer Coco Chanel turned the simple sweaters into high fashion.

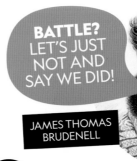

BATTLE? LET'S JUST NOT AND SAY WE DID!

JAMES THOMAS BRUDENELL

I ONCE RULED THE **RUNWAY!**

Bet You **Didn't Know**

Michelle Obama, the first lady of the United States at the time, made cardigans trendy in 2009 when she wore them on TV during interviews and to official outings.

KILLER Clothing

I n the 19th century, getting dressed and ready in the morning could be downright deadly. People yearned to meet a certain set of beauty standards (pale skin, rosy cheeks, and a thin waist) and were willing to risk their lives in the name of looking good.

Treacherous Toppers

In this era, no man wanted to appear in public without wearing a hat—it was unseemly. That proved to be unfortunate for the hatters who earned a living making them: The process involved brushing fur pelts with mercury to turn them into felt. Unfortunately, mercury is a highly toxic substance that can cause brain damage. The practice gave rise to the phrase "mad as a hatter."

HOOPS-IE DAISY!

TALK ABOUT A KILLER LOOK!

Menacing Makeup

For Victorian women, perhaps the most dangerous act of their day was sitting down to apply their makeup. White skin was prized at the time, so women often painted on makeup laced with lead, which was both white and toxic. As a final touch, some would put drops of the deadly poison nightshade in their eyes to make their pupils dilated, or larger, which was thought to be extremely attractive.

Death Becomes Her

In the 1800s, people didn't know that many diseases were caused by germs. When tuberculosis, a lung infection, spread into an epidemic, Victorians romanticized what they saw as the disease's eye-catching side effects: Its victims were rosy-cheeked and red-lipped from fever, and their waists shrunk to tiny proportions as they wasted away. Healthy women wore corsets and makeup to mimic the effects.

Flammable Fashion

Women during this time sported wide hoop skirts made of yards of fabric. The style wasn't the most practical choice, considering all the candles, oil lamps, and fireplaces that people used for light and heat in the days before electricity. In fact, it could be downright dangerous. It was common for women to suffer severe burns or die when their outfits went up in flames.

Deadly Dye

In the Victorian age, the chemical element arsenic was used to dye dresses, gloves, shoes, and flower wreaths a bright shade of green. But the substance was so toxic that it could cause death in people who were exposed to it for too long. Nevertheless, many Victorian women took regular small doses to lighten their skin—which was then viewed as attractive.

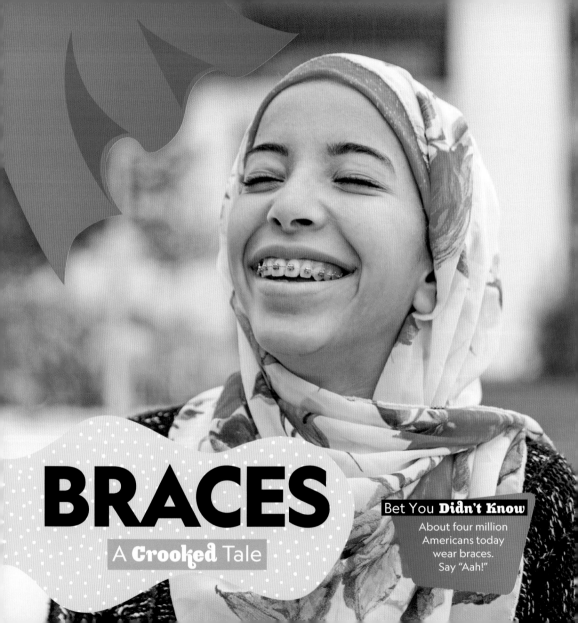

BRACES

A **Crooked** Tale

If you've ever sat in an orthodontist's chair and held your mouth open as metal wires were torturously tightened around your teeth, you might have thought: Whose idea was this?

Modern braces—stainless-steel brackets affixed to each tooth and strung together by a wire—date back to the early 1800s. But people have been concerned about crooked smiles since long before that. Archaeologists have dug up ancient Egyptian mummies with crude metal bands around their teeth. Experts think these might have been similar to the brackets of modern braces, with string made from cat intestines used for the tightening wire.

After the ancient Egyptians, there wasn't much progress in the field of orthodontics for more than 17 centuries. Then, a Frenchman named

PUT ON A **HAPPY FACE!**

PIERRE FAUCHARD

Pierre Fauchard, who is considered the father of dentistry, came up with several devices for straightening teeth, including a horseshoe-shaped strip of metal called a bandeau with holes that fit around the teeth to move them into alignment.

But a straight smile didn't become widely popular until the 20th century. Then, the medical minds of the age finally figured out that diets high in sugar and processed flour caused cavities. As their teeth stopped falling out, people started to want an ever more perfect grin. The field of orthodontics was born, along with all kinds of devices for shifting, nudging, and pulling teeth straight into submission.

THESE STRINGS WERE **MADE OF WHAT?!**

HOODIES

A **Peek** Under the Hood

They're the outerwear of choice for skaters and hip-hop artists, so it might seem like the hoodie is the ultimate symbol of modern street wear. But who was really hiding under history's first hoodies?

Some of the earliest evidence of hooded garments comes from ancient Greece and Rome. In the Middle Ages, monks dressed in cape-like garments with hoods attached. But the hoodie's ancestors had darker associations, too: It was the outfit depicted on the Grim Reaper, the shrouded symbol of death that emerged during the plague that killed one-third of Europeans in the 14th century.

The modern hoodie, a garment usually made of cotton, often with a kangaroo-like pocket in the front, was invented in the 1930s. It was first intended to keep athletes warm. But soon, those who worked in cold conditions, such as employees laboring in refrigerated storage units or outside in cold temps, slipped on the sweatshirts and pulled up the hoods.

Around the mid-1970s, the hoodie went from practical garment to fashion statement when hip-hop culture was born on the streets of New York City. Skateboarders wore them while sneaking into empty parking garages to practice tricks, and graffiti artists could hide inside their hoods to stay anonymous. The hoodie's rebellious reputation has lasted to the modern day. Even some CEOs bypass traditional suits in favor of the cool, counterculture—and comfortable—hoodie!

I MAKE GRIM LOOK GOOD!

I AM READY TO **STRUT MY STUFF!**

Bet You **Didn't Know**

In the 1990s, hoodies hit the runway when high-fashion designers started making their own versions.

71

CHANGING Clothes

When you get dressed in the morning, you might reach for your softest sweatshirt or your jeans that fit just right. But for thousands of years, people didn't have many options—they had to use what was close at hand to cover up. Here's how clothing materials have changed over time.

GO AHEAD, TAKE A WHIFF!

People started spinning wool, the hair of sheep, into cloth around 9000 B.C. It makes such warm fabric that we're still wearing it today. Wool is naturally bacteria-resistant, meaning that it can be worn repeatedly without starting to smell. In 2013, one manufacturer of woolen clothing proved the point by wearing a wool shirt for 100 days straight, then inviting customers to take a whiff!

9000 B.C.
Wool

20,000 B.C.   15,000 B.C.   10,000 B.C.

20,000 B.C.
Leaves, Fur, and Leather

In warm climates, early hominids made fabrics from large leaves or grasses. In chilly places, they used animal skins. At first, the material was held together with fish bones and thorns and then, around 20,000 B.C., by sewing. At about the same time, people discovered how to turn hides into leather by curing them with a noxious substance that included animal brains.

6500 B.C.
Linen

Living under the hot African sun, the ancient Egyptians needed something cool and light to wear. They collected wild flax plants from the banks of the Nile river, dried them, and separated the stems into fibers, which could be woven into a lightweight fabric called linen. Even the dead wore it: Mummies were wrapped in hundreds of yards of linen strips.

3000 B.C.
Silk

Around 5,000 years ago, the people of China discovered that the cocoon of the silkworm could be unraveled into one strong filament as long as 3,000 feet (900 m). They closely guarded the secret of their luxury fabric for centuries. It wasn't until A.D. 552 that two monks smuggled silkworm eggs into Europe, setting off a worldwide silk craze.

A.D. 1883
Synthetic Fabric

People had tried to make artificial fabrics that mimicked linen, cotton, or silk for centuries before British inventor Sir Joseph Swan accidentally hit on the first human-made fiber while searching for a filament for his lightbulb, in 1883. But it took until the 1890s for a reliable method of manufacturing the stuff, called rayon, to be invented. After that came a whole host of human-made fabrics, from nylon to polyester.

5000 B.C.   A.D. 1   2000

3000 B.C.
Cotton

Historians believe ancient people in the part of the Indus Valley that was in modern-day India were the first to grow the cotton plant, and they loved the soft fabric they could make from the fibers. When cotton was exported to Europe around 63 B.C., Europeans went crazy for it, too. The first European cotton industries, in Barcelona, Spain, made sails used to power boats that carried goods around the world.

RAIN BOOTS

Splish-Splash Shoes

J umping in puddles after a rainstorm is a beloved wet-weather activity. But it would be much less pleasant without rain boots to keep your feet from getting soaked!

It's fitting that this protective footwear was likely first developed in the rainiest place on Earth—the rainforest. The first European visitors to the thick Amazon jungle reported that the indigenous people there had boots made of a mysterious squishy, waterproof substance: rubber. No one is sure exactly how they made the boots, but historians believe they dipped their feet in the sap of a special tree, held this early rubber over the fire to harden, and repeated the process again and again over many hours. Yowch!

Modern rain boots were the brainchild of American chemist and engineer Charles Goodyear. Goodyear imagined a world in which everything was made of rubber. But his early attempts cracked in the cold and melted in the heat. In 1839, he accidentally

Bet You **Didn't Know**

For many years, Yorkshire, England, U.K., had a "wellie wanging" world championship, where competitors would "wang" (Yorkshire for "throw") a boot as far as they could.

invented a more durable version when he spilled a concoction of rubber, sulfur, and white lead onto a hot stove, creating chemically hardened, or vulcanized, rubber.

Around the same time in the United Kingdom, the Duke of Wellington asked his shoemaker to make him a simple, low-heeled, knee-high boot. The result was known as the Wellington, and it became famous among the British aristocracy. In the mid-19th century, Goodyear's vulcanization process was used to make the first rubber Wellingtons. They became so popular that in rainy Britain, where the boots are a necessity, they're still called wellies today.

CHARLES GOODYEAR

BASEBALL **CAPS**

Today, you don't have to be a player—or even a fan—to sport one, but baseball caps got their start on the field. Before the first cap was introduced in 1858, baseball players wore something no modern athlete would dream of donning—straw hats!

The straw hat, introduced by the New York Knickerbocker Base Ball Club in 1849, didn't offer much in the way of protection from the sun. But because it was considered improper for a man to appear hatless in public in the 1800s, the players put up with them. That changed over the next century, when people started spending more time in cars, where hats just got in the way.

By 1953, players were wearing modern-style baseball caps—and the stands were full of cap-wearing fans. But it took until the late 1970s for people to start wearing them anywhere else besides at the game. One reason was the explosion of televised sports. Fans loved wearing their team's hat

wherever they were watching the game.

Sporting News magazine started selling baseball caps via mail order in 1979, and suddenly people were wearing them for fashion, not just fandom. Today, people show personal style by wearing their caps tilted at an angle, bent across the brim, or artfully frayed at the edges.

HMM, SOMETHING FEELS **OFF!**

Bet You **Didn't Know**

In 2017, baseball great Jackie Robinson's 1946 cap sold for $590,994.

AS IT **SHOULD!**

SEWING
MACHINES

Sew **Useful**

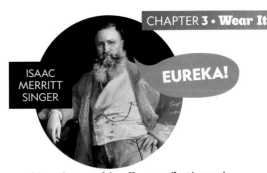

ISAAC MERRITT SINGER

EUREKA!

If it weren't for needle and thread, we'd all be walking around with no clothes. Every piece of clothing, from your shirt to your socks, has to be stitched together. And until the sewing machine came along, it had to be done by hand.

More than 20,000 years ago, early humans used needles made of bone or animal horns and thread made of tendons. By about A.D. 200, people in ancient China were using thimbles to help them push needles through thick material such as animal hides.

Needle and thread remained the only way to sew for centuries before a workable machine took over. Would-be inventors tried out different ideas through the 1700s and early 1800s, but all of them failed. That's because of a puzzling problem: Nobody could figure out how to make a machine that could pull a needle through from one side of the fabric to the other, like human hands can.

The person who finally came up with the solution was Isaac Singer, a former actor, ditchdigger, and cabinetmaker who struck success with his Singer sewing machine. It used an up-and-down needle motion, along with a special stitch copped from another inventor, to make a neat seam. Some people wanted a Singer of their own so badly that they coughed up $125 for a single machine—in a time when the average American income was just $500 a year!

SEW WE ARE NOW POINTLESS!

Bet You Didn't Know

Polar explorer Richard Byrd brought six Singer sewing machines along with him to Antarctica. You never know when you'll split a seam!

CHAPTER 4

Health & Medicine

Until the birth of modern medicine, doctors thought nothing of performing back-to-back surgeries with the same dirty instruments—or even prescribing their patients ointment made of animal poop! It's no wonder that many medical technologies, from microscopes to vitamins, have bizarre backstories.

ANESTHESIA

A **Knockout** Story

Bet You **Didn't Know**

Before the advent of anesthesia, doctors tried all kinds of pain-killing techniques, such as rubbing the patient with stinging nettles to distract them or knocking them unconscious with a blow to the jaw.

If the idea of surgery is unsettling to you, imagine going under the knife in the 18th century. Before the invention of anesthesia, patients had to remain fully conscious. Operations were so painful and terrifying that they were only performed as a last resort.

That meant that the most important skill a surgeon could have was speed. British physician Robert Liston was famously able to remove a leg in less than 30 seconds. His accuracy wasn't as impressive: Liston once sliced off three of his assistant's fingers and slashed a hole in an onlooker's coat.

But on October 16, 1846, at Massachusetts General Hospital in the United States, a young dentist named William Morton publicly anesthetized a young male patient. Morton then removed a tumor on the left side of the patient's jaw. The man didn't scream or struggle during the operation, much to the surprise of the breathless onlookers.

That first anesthetic was a colorless gas called ether. Morton put his life on the line in the name of discovering the secret to surgery without pain: He inhaled the fumes himself to test the safety! But ether proved unpredictable: Sometimes the patient died on the table, or—horrifyingly—woke up mid-surgery. Anesthetics didn't become popular until 1853, when Britain's Queen Victoria used one called chloroform to ease the pain of giving birth to her eighth child.

WILLIAM MORTON

NO PAIN, ALL GAIN!

ETHER

ANTISEPTICS

Begone, **Bacteria**

Even if you survived the terrible pain of 18th-century surgery without anesthesia (page 82), the worst was often yet to come. Surgeons didn't wash their hands before operations and carried the same blood-encrusted instruments from one procedure to the next. So it's not surprising that up to 50 percent of all hospital patients died of infection.

People had known about the tiny living things we now call germs, or microorganisms, since the 1670s. But Victorian doctors didn't think they had anything to do with getting sick. Instead, they believed that disease was spread by poisonous air called "miasma."

Proof that they had been on the wrong track came from French biologist Louis Pasteur. Pasteur showed that if he boiled broth to kill off any microorganisms and then immediately sealed the container, it would stay clear. But if he left it open, the broth would turn cloudy because microorganisms in the air would fall inside and grow. Pasteur knew that the same process must be how disease could spread from the sick to the healthy. But nobody believed him—except for a young British surgeon named Joseph Lister.

LOUIS PASTEUR

CLOUDY WITH A CHANCE OF **YUCK!**

On August 12, 1865, an 11-year-old boy with a wound from a severe bone fracture was carried into Lister's hospital. For the first time in history, Lister cleaned and covered the wound with bacteria-killing carbolic acid, then crossed his fingers. The wound healed without infection, and six weeks later, the boy walked out of the hospital. It was the beginning of a medical revolution.

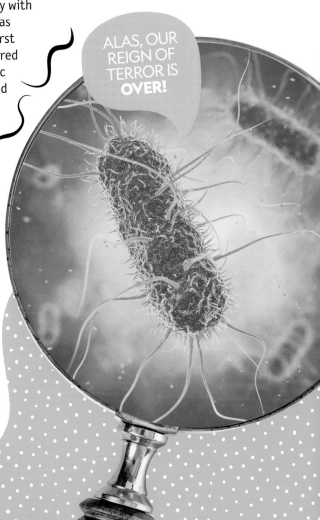

ALAS, OUR REIGN OF TERROR IS **OVER!**

Bet You **Didn't Know**

Though Lister did not invent the mouthwash Listerine, his innovations inspired its invention.

AND THAT IS HOW YOU **KILL BACTERIA!**

LISTERINE
COOL MINT

MOUTHWASH

Reduces Plaque and Removes up to 97% of Germs Left Behind After Brushing

500 ml ℮

VACCINE

A Little **Pinch**

Less than a century ago, millions of people were killed every year by diseases like whooping cough and diphtheria. Yet today they're fairly rare in many parts of the world. What changed?

People have been trying to prevent disease for centuries. In 11th-century China, a disease called smallpox was killing people left and right. In an attempt to keep from getting sick, healthy people took scabs from the infected blisters of the sick and stuck them inside their noses. One in 50 people died from the practice, but a few of the survivors became immune.

By the 18th century, people in England had realized that milkmaids who caught cowpox (a disease similar to smallpox that makes cows sick but only causes mild blisters in humans) became immune to smallpox. On May 14, 1796, an English doctor named Edward Jenner collected fluid from a cowpox blister and scratched it into the skin of an eight-year-old boy, purposefully infecting him with the cowpox virus. On July 1, Jenner once again infected his patient with a virus—but this time, it was smallpox. The boy stayed perfectly healthy. Exposure to cowpox had protected him from the related disease of smallpox.

In the 19th and 20th centuries, scientists used the principle Jenner had discovered to develop vaccines to fight all kinds of deadly diseases, such as polio, yellow fever, and typhus. By 1980, smallpox had been wiped off the face of the planet. Several more diseases are now close to being totally elimi-nated in the United States.

EDWARD JENNER

COWPOX! HOW DAIRY YOU!

Bet You **Didn't Know**

As early as the seventh century, monks in India drank snake venom in an attempt to make them-selves immune to snake-bites. (It didn't work.)

Ouch!
MEDICAL INSTRUMENTS FROM THE PAST

If you think these look like instruments of torture, you're not far off. They're ancient medical instruments. But they often caused more suffering than they prevented.

Bullet Extractor

As soldiers shifted from waging wars with swords and battle-axes to firearms, army doctors were faced with a new kind of battlefield injury: embedded bullets. Invented in the 1500s, bullet extractors like this one had a hollow tube containing a long screw. Turning the central handle would extend a metal tip that would pierce the bullet so it could be pulled out.

THE KEY TO **HEALTHY TEETH!**

Dental Key

You really didn't want to get a toothache in the days of yore. The most common treatment for a diseased tooth was to simply yank it out—with no numbing painkillers. In the 18th century, the dental key was the tool of choice for the operation. The dentist—sometimes called a barber-surgeon—would grasp the tooth in the claw, then turn the key until the force levered it out.

Jedi Helmet

In the 1980s, MRI (magnetic resonance imaging) scanning—which uses a magnetic field and radio waves to create pictures of the inside of the body—was a brand-new technology. Early machines weren't powerful enough to get a clear image of children's smaller brains, so researchers created this copper-wrapped headgear to boost the signal. They called them "Jedi helmets" to encourage nervous kids to wear them.

Lancet

For at least 3,000 years, one of the most popular treatments for many ailments was to remove some of the patient's blood. Of course, now we know that except in a few rare cases, bloodletting doesn't cure the problem and leaves a sick person much weaker. But as late as the 19th century, a visit to the doctor would mean having a vein cut open with a sharp lancet.

I CAME, **I SAW,** I CONQUERED!

Surgical Saw

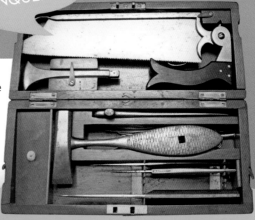

If you had an infected wound in the time before antiseptics (page 84), often your best hope of survival was amputation. Surgeons of the past would use saws like this one to cut through bone. In the 1600s, they were often covered with decorative ridges and patterns, a status symbol that showed off the skill of the doctor. Unfortunately, the crevices were the perfect place for bacteria to grow. Oops.

HEARING AIDS

How's That?

As far back as the 13th century, if a person with hearing loss wanted to listen to someone speaking, the options were awkward. They had to hold huge funnel-shaped devices to their ears and point them toward the person they were trying to hear.

Around the 16th century, people experimented with carving wooden hearing aids into the shape of animals known for their exceptional hearing. (Imagine donning your giant rabbit-ear hearing aid at a party.) During the 17th and 18th centuries, these evolved into the ear trumpet, with a horn-shaped piece at one end to collect sound tapering into a thin tube to direct the sound into the ear. But none of these early models amplified sound by much.

During the 1800s, concealed hearing aids became fashionable. They were built into shirt collars or designed to be hidden in a full beard. The throne of the king of Portugal, John VI, had hollow arm rests in the shape of roaring lions. Hidden inside were ear trumpets which directed sound through tubes up the back of the throne to the king's ears. King John had his subjects kneel when speaking to him, so their mouths were level with the animal heads—never revealing he had hearing loss.

When the telephone buzzed onto the scene in 1876, many inventors tried to modify it into the first electric hearing aid. But the batteries ran out quickly and the devices were large and bulky. One from 1907 was the size of a file cabinet! Since then, miniaturization of technology has shrunk hearing aids down so that some sit right inside the ear canal. Now that's a sound idea!

I CAN HEAR **YOU!**

PROSTHETICS

Artificial **Appendages**

THESE FIT **PAW-FECTLY!**

OSCAR THE BIONIC CAT

In 2017, archaeologists were excavating a tomb near Luxor, Egypt, when they found something surprising: a big toe. The toe, which was made of wood and leather, dated back to around 1000 B.C., making it the world's oldest known prosthetic body part.

Most ancient imitation body parts were just for looks. But experts think that the Egyptian toe was a functional replacement for one of the real big toes, which carry about 40 percent of a person's body weight and help propel them forward. Later, artificial limbs from the medieval period allowed knights who had lost their limbs to continue to fight. Prosthetic hands often had hinged fingers that could hold reins or grasp a shield.

A huge boom in prosthetic technology came about from the American Civil War, fought from 1861 to 1865. Battlefield doctors, overwhelmed with injured patients and harried by wartime conditions, didn't have time for delicate procedures like splinting limbs, so they often simply

removed them instead. About 45,000 amputations were performed during the war. But prosthetic options were so primitive that many of the amputees took to designing their own. One, Samuel Decker, created his own advanced prosthetic arms with attachments— including a spoon—to help him perform everyday activities.

SAMUEL DECKER

After World War I, innovative prosthetics allowed people to perform tasks that were impossible before, such as welding metal or driving a car. But they were nothing compared to today's next-generation prosthetics. In 2018, a man named Johnny Matheny who had lost his arm to cancer became the first person to live with an advanced prosthetic that can be controlled using the brain. Just by thinking, Matheny can rotate his wrist and move his fingers. He hopes to someday even play the piano.

ANYTHING IS **POSSIBLE.**

Bet You **Didn't Know**

New 3D printing technology is enabling people to download and print prosthetic limbs for less than $50, compared to a traditional prosthesis, which might cost tens of thousands of dollars.

MICROSCOPES

Zooming In

When the microscope was invented, it showed people a miniature world they had never imagined existed. Tiny creatures swam, wiggled, and crawled in our food and water and on every surface. Few inventions have rocked science more.

The earliest microscope, created in the 1600s, was a simple tube with a plate for the object to be studied on one end, and a lens, or curved piece of glass, at the other end. The lens was only powerful enough to magnify the object by 10 times. But people were still transfixed by the up-close view they got of insects, nicknaming the device "flea glasses."

Seventeenth-century scientists became convinced that the microscope could unlock the mysteries of the universe. In 1665, British scientist Robert Hooke figured out how to reconfigure the microscope's lenses to make one that could magnify by 30 times. He peered at plant slivers and found that they were full of tiny chambers, estimating that one square inch (6.5 sq cm) of cork would contain 1,259,712,000 of them. That made him the first person to describe cells.

A decade later, members of London's Royal Society of scientists started receiving reports from a poorly educated merchant in Holland named Antonie van Leeuwenhoek. He had managed to teach himself the art of crafting glass lenses with perfect clarity, enabling him to magnify objects up to 275 times. Over the next 50 years, he sent up-close detailed drawings of almost everything he could examine, from bread mold to his own saliva. We haven't looked at the world the same way since.

FINALLY, THE ATTENTION I **DESERVE!**

A WHOLE NEW **WOOORLD!**

ANTONIE VAN LEEUWENHOEK

STRANGE
Remedies

Nobody likes going to the doctor. But in ancient times, it wasn't just annoying—it could be life-threatening. In a time before modern science, doctors were often left to their best guesses when it came to treating sick people. And some of the treatments they came up with were truly bizarre.

WHO NEEDS ASPIRIN?!

Maggots and Leeches

Applying maggots or leeches to wounds was once common all over the world. Surprisingly, this ancient treatment is now making a comeback. Modern science has found that maggots and leeches are remarkably proficient at eating away the dead tissue from certain wounds and leaving healthy living tissue behind, preventing infection. But don't try this at home!

Like a Hole in the Head

Archaeologists have unearthed thousands of ancient human skulls bearing a gruesome wound: a hole cut there deliberately. Trepanation is the oldest form of surgery in human history, performed as far back as 7,000 years ago. Some experts think it was a ritual practice meant to let evil spirits out of the body; others think it was used to treat medical problems like chronic headaches.

Moldy Bread

More than 2,000 years ago, all kinds of ancient people didn't trash moldy bread; they pressed it against wounds and skin infections. It might sound crazy, but now we know that certain fungi can block the growth of disease-causing bacteria. So this is one ancient cure that could have worked.

DO YOUR WORST, **PLAGUE!**

I'M HERE TO **HELP!**

Poo Prescription

In some ways, ancient Egyptian doctors were far ahead of their time, even recommending that patients wash their bodies to prevent infection. In other ways, they were way off. One of ancient Egypt's most common remedies for diseases and injuries was dung. Donkey, dog, gazelle, and fly feces were all thought to be excellent treatments for all kinds of conditions.

A Cloud of Protection

When modern people pass gas, they want it to go unnoticed. But in the Middle Ages, they tried to capture it in a jar and save it for later. Between 1665 and 1666, the Great Plague of London killed about 100,000 people. Because it was airborne, people thought the plague's deadly vapors could be counteracted by deadly vapors of their own. When plague appeared in their neighborhood, they opened the jar and inhaled the fumes to ward off disease.

THERMOMETER

Today, you might check the day's temperature to help you decide whether to put on a warm coat when you leave the house. But before the invention of the thermometer, you just had to stick your arm out the window and make your best guess.

Air and water both expand and contract with temperature changes. In 1592, Italian scientist Galileo Galilei used this phenomenon to make a long, thin glass tube with a bulb on one end. Galileo would heat the bulb to expand the air inside. Then he would turn the instrument over and immerse it in water. If the temperature of the bulb lowered, it would decrease the pressure of the air inside and suck water into the tube. The higher the water level, the colder the temperature.

Any tiny flaw in a thermometer's glass tube would cause an inaccurate reading. But making perfect glass tubes in a time when everything was made by hand proved very tough. The person to crack the problem was a German-born instrument-maker named Daniel Gabriel Fahrenheit, who made the first accurate thermometer in 1717. But for reasons that are still a mystery, Fahrenheit calibrated the instrument so that 32 degrees was water's freezing point and 212 its boiling point.

Shortly after, a Swedish competitor named Anders Celsius came up with a new scale that put the freezing point at 0 and the boiling point at 100. Today, only the United States and a few other countries continue to stick to the Fahrenheit system.

ANDERS CELSIUS

AND THAT'S **A PERFECT SCALE.**

Bet You **Didn't Know**

At sea level, water boils at 212 degrees Fahrenheit (100°C). But at the top of Mount Everest, water boils at 159.8 degrees Fahrenheit (71°C) because the lower the air pressure, the lower the temperature at which water boils.

VITAMINS

Edible **Alphabet**

For most of seafaring history, the scourge of the seven seas wasn't pirates or shipwrecks—it was scurvy. Its death toll could be shocking: On one three-year voyage in the 1740s, a British naval expedition lost 1,400 men out of 2,000. Four were killed in battle. Nearly all the rest died of scurvy.

Sailors who came down with the disease would grow weak and suffer from aching limbs. Soon, they would begin to bleed under the skin, their vision would blur, and their teeth would fall out. Miraculously, when sailors got to port and ate fresh food, they recovered. But why? In the mid-1700s, James Lind, a surgeon in the British Royal Navy, did an experiment. He gave sailors with scurvy different foods, including vinegar, garlic and mustard, and oranges and lemons. The sailors who got the citrus made a swift recovery. Unfortunately, Lind ignored his finding in favor of his personal belief that scurvy was caused by food that wasn't digested all the way.

The true cause of scurvy is a lack of ascorbic acid, also called vitamin C—a molecule found in citrus. But it took a very long time for people to realize that an inadequate diet could cause disease. They had clues, such as the 1897 discovery that people in Java who ate white rice (which has had its outer layer polished away) often got a life-threatening nerve disease called beriberi, while people who ate whole-grain rice did not. Fifteen years later, researchers figured out the reason: White rice was missing a molecule called thiamine. It was

IS IT THE LEMONS? **NAH!**

JAMES LIND

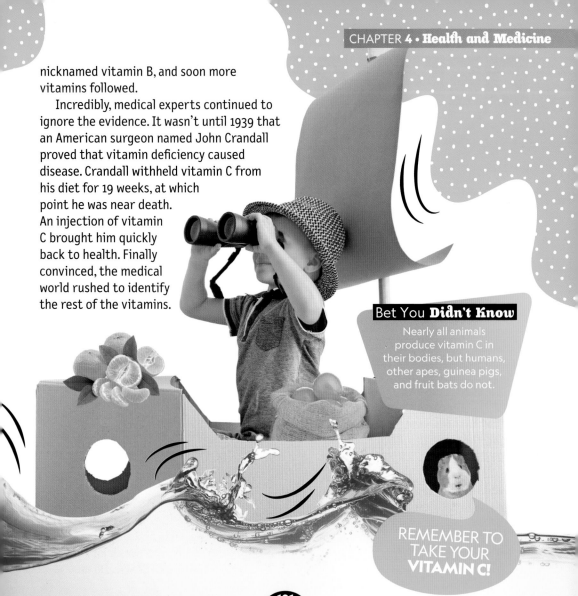

nicknamed vitamin B, and soon more vitamins followed.

Incredibly, medical experts continued to ignore the evidence. It wasn't until 1939 that an American surgeon named John Crandall proved that vitamin deficiency caused disease. Crandall withheld vitamin C from his diet for 19 weeks, at which point he was near death. An injection of vitamin C brought him quickly back to health. Finally convinced, the medical world rushed to identify the rest of the vitamins.

Bet You Didn't Know

Nearly all animals produce vitamin C in their bodies, but humans, other apes, guinea pigs, and fruit bats do not.

REMEMBER TO TAKE YOUR **VITAMIN C!**

DEFIBRILLATOR

A Shocking **Story**

You might have noticed cases the size of a lunch box on the walls of airports, malls, and train stations. They're fronted with break-in-case-of-emergency glass and have a mysterious device inside. That device is a defibrillator, used to shock a heart whose beat has gone awry back into its normal rhythm.

When it's working correctly, the human heart is a miraculous machine. Electrical impulses move through the muscle cells of the heart's four chambers, causing them to contract in a rhythm as regular as a ticking clock, pumping blood through the body. But if something goes wrong with the electrical current, the heart beats out of rhythm and the person can die.

In the early 1900s, workmen installing electric lines occasionally died after accidental shocks. While running experiments to test what made electric current lethal, engineers noticed

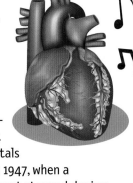

ELECTRO-MEDICAL
MACHINE, 1850s

that shocks could sometimes restart dogs' hearts after they had been electrocuted. That caught the attention of an American heart surgeon named Claude Beck, who began conducting his own experiments in the basement of the University Hospitals of Cleveland, in Ohio. In 1947, when a 14-year-old patient's heart stopped during surgery, two shocks from Beck's experimental device brought the boy back to life.

Beck's model was so primitive it used two tablespoons to deliver the zap. But the design has come a long way: Today's models use simple voice directions to tell rescuers what to do. It's estimated that they help bystanders save about 1,700 lives every year in the United States alone.

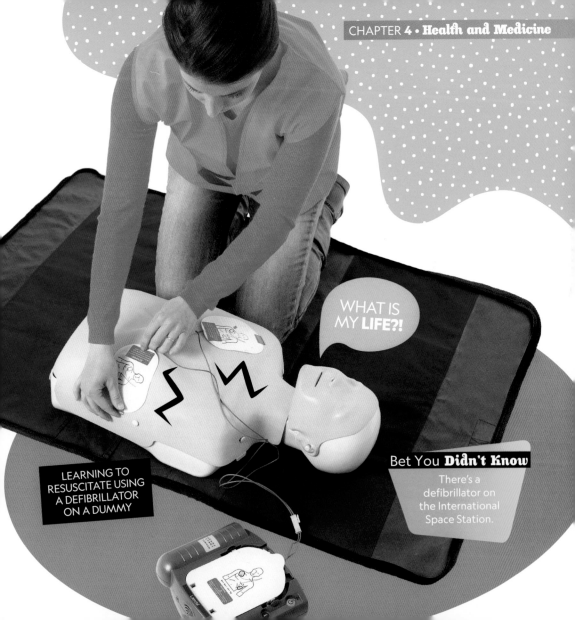

WHAT IS MY **LIFE**?!

LEARNING TO RESUSCITATE USING A DEFIBRILLATOR ON A DUMMY

Bet You **Didn't Know**
There's a defibrillator on the International Space Station.

CHAPTER 5

Fabulous Food

There's nothing surprising about pizza, cheese, or corn ... or is there? Bite into the origins of everyday foods, and you might find a surprise inside. Some dishes don't come from where you might expect. Others changed the course of world history. All are truly incredible edibles.

PIZZA

A Slice of **History**

Whether you like deep dish or thin crust, there's no denying pizza is one of the world's favorite foods. But you might be surprised that the original pizza pies were a battle-field snack.

People have been chewing on pizza's precursors for thousands of years. The ancient Greeks often snacked on flatbreads topped with vegetables and flavored with herbs and spices. Around the fifth or sixth century B.C., Persian foot soldiers baked on-the-go flatbreads on their shields, and they covered them with cheese and dates.

Many consider Naples, Italy, to be the birthplace of modern pizza. In A.D. 79, a volcanic eruption from nearby Mount Vesuvius buried part of that city, as well as completely destroying nearby Pompeii. Under the rubble and ash, archaeologists discovered an ancient bakery that looked much like a modern pizzeria. Back then, pizza was a favorite food of Naples's

working class, sold by street vendors and topped with garnishes still popular today, such as tomatoes, cheese, oil, anchovies, and garlic.

Pizza's reputation as a food for the poor changed when Italy's King Umberto I and Queen Margherita visited Naples in 1889. Bored with royal feasting, the pair decided to try the food of the people and ordered an assortment of pizzas. The queen was especially taken with a version topped with mozzarella, tomatoes, and basil, known forever after as pizza Margherita. When Italians immigrated to the United States in the late 19th and early 20th centuries, they brought this trendy pizza with them, and it's been the standard pie ever since.

CHEESED TO MEET YOU!

QUEEN MARGHERITA

CHEESE THE DAY!

Bet You Didn't Know

At the annual World Pizza Games, competitors face off in categories like acrobatic dough tossing and fastest pizza box folding.

107

CHEESE

Milk Magic

Soft, hard, creamy, or stinky—many people have a favorite cheese. But for people of the past, cheese wasn't a treat—it was a matter of survival.

Experts once believed that wheels of cheese first rolled onto the scene in medieval times. But in 2012, archaeologists made a discovery that blew that timeline away: prehistoric pottery from Poland that was pierced with a series of small holes—just like the modern strainers used in the cheese-making process. Sure enough, traces of ancient milk residue were found on the artifacts. That discovery put the birth of cheese back to 7,000 years ago.

Those early humans did not have the ability to digest the sugars in milk, called lactose. That meant they couldn't use the milk of cows, goats, and sheep for nutrition. But they could eat cheese, which is much lower in lactose. So experts think

THE MOLD AND THE BRIE-TIFUL!

ancient people started making cheese as a way to take advantage of a new source of nutrition. As they incorporated the milk product into their diet, over many generations some people's bodies became so adept at digesting lactose that they could drink milk itself without suffering digestive distress. Today, about 35 percent of the world population can digest dairy products with no trouble.

CHEESE PRODUCTION

Ancient cheese was probably a similar consistency to today's cottage cheese. As different cultures started making cheese for themselves, the results they got varied depending on the types of bacteria that were floating around in their environment. Today, there are more than 1,400 types of cheese you can choose from to make your grilled cheese sandwich.

WHAT A **NIGHT!**

Bet You **Didn't Know**

A wheel of cheese weighing more than 1,000 pounds (454 kg) was given to Britain's Queen Victoria as a wedding gift.

CHILI
DOG
One **Packed** Pup

WE ARE SO **PROUD!**

POLAND · GREECE · MEXICO

A soft, squishy bun. A steaming frank. A scoopful of chili. A handful of cheddar cheese. The chili dog is an iconic all-American treat. But it has surprisingly diverse origins.

In the 1890s, a wave of Eastern European immigrants moved to the United States and opened businesses, including many butcher shops selling the sausages of their native lands. Americans were suspicious of the foreign food, driving up demand for mass-produced sausages made in U.S. factories. The modern hot dog was born.

Then there's the chili sauce: In the 1870s, women from Mexico came to San Antonio, Texas, set up booths, and started selling sauce made with ground meat. These "Chili Queens" disappeared by the mid-1900s, but their sauce stuck around in the form of *chili con carne*, a staple of Tex-Mex cuisine.

By the 1880s, it was being mass-produced and sold in cans—another immigrant food turned into an American staple.

The chili found on chili dogs today often includes ingredients like cinnamon and oregano—seasonings that hail from Macedonia and Greece. Immigrants from these countries came to the American Midwest in the early 1900s, where many made a living as foodsellers. To make the spice-spiked sauces of their homelands seem more familiar to Americans, they ladled them over hot dogs, serving up the world's first chili dogs. So the next time you grab one (don't forget the napkins!), take a moment to marvel at the cultural mishmash hiding inside the bun.

Bet You **Didn't Know**

Different regions of the U.S. each have their own version of the chili dog, from the "Texas wiener" to the "Cheese coneys" of Cincinnati, Ohio.

NOT-SO-FAMILIAR
Fruits and Veggies

You can probably identify apples, corn, and watermelon at the grocery store without looking at the labels. But go back in time a few thousand years and you'd have a hard time finding any fruits and veggies that looked familiar. Thousands of years of careful growing has changed them to look nothing like their ancestors.

Bananas

Imagine slicing this banana. The wild plants *Musa acuminata* and *Musa balbisiana* were first cultivated as early as 10,000 years ago in what is now Papua New Guinea. Over time, they became the long, soft version with tiny seeds we know today. But the original *Musa balbisiana* had little flesh and large, hard seeds.

Carrots

You would have been disappointed to pull a carrot out of the ground in the 10th century. Purple or white and in a thin, branching shape, they looked more like an unappetizing root than a delectable vegetable. As they were cultivated, likely by the ancient Greeks and Romans, they became larger, sweeter, and took on an orange hue (though you can find purple and white varieties today).

WE ARE SO FULL OF **VITAMINS!**

Corn

It took scientists a long time to figure out where corn came from. That's because it was bred from a kind of Mexican grass called teosinte. Teosinte's skinny ears, with just a few dozen hard kernels each, are hard for humans to digest, even when boiled or mashed. But they could be popped—and popcorn was the original way people ate this plant about 7,000 years ago.

Peaches

Small with a large pit, ancient wild peaches looked more like today's cherries. First domesticated around 4000 B.C. by the Chinese, they weren't sweet and fruity, but earthy and slightly salty. Today's peaches are 64 times larger and 27 percent juicier. And 100 percent better in pie, probably.

JUST **PEACHY!**

IT ISN'T **SUMMER** WITHOUT ME!

Watermelon

People have been gnawing on watermelon for at least 5,000 years, judging from the seeds found at an ancient site in Libya. Paintings of watermelons have been discovered in ancient Egyptian tombs, including the tomb of King Tutankhamun. But judging from the art, they looked very different from modern melons, with less flesh and lots of seeds. There must have been much more spitting!

BREAD

The Loaf of Life

It seems like no big deal when you pop a slice in the toaster. But bread in all its forms—from Indian naan to a French baguette—is the most widely consumed food in the world. And it's been an essential part of the human diet for a very long time.

ASSORTED NAAN

In 2015, archaeologists were exploring an ancient cave in southern Italy that was once home to prehistoric people when they found a clue to the past. Clinging to a blunt rock were ancient grains that had been baked and ground in the same process we use to make flour today—but they were 30,000 years old!

Early carb lovers probably ground down wild plant roots a bit like potatoes to make flour. Then they added water and baked the mixture on hot stones into a kind of flatbread. Breads in this style, such as Mexican tortillas and Jewish matzo, are still around today. The first risen bread probably happened by accident, when yeast spores floated into a batch of dough and caused it to expand. By 300 B.C., the ancient Egyptians had bakeries that made enough loaves to feed the pyramid builders.

Bread spread across the world. In 19th-century Britain, it was so important to the human diet that people ate very little else. A typical daily diet for a lower-income family was a bit of tea and sugar, a few vegetables, and a slice or two of cheese—all the rest was bread.

Bet You **Didn't Know**

Bread was used as a form of currency in ancient Egypt.

I GOT **DOUGH** (LITERALLY)!

POTATOES

Stupendous Spuds

Some would say that no Thanksgiving spread is complete without a mound of buttery mashed potatoes, and that every burger needs a side of fries. Potatoes are a cooking staple—and without them, the modern world wouldn't be the same.

Potatoes originated in the Andes mountains on South America's Pacific coast. Active volcanoes, earthquakes, floods, landslides, and a climate that can swing from fair to freezing in hours make the Andes no easy place to make a living. Yet 8,000 years ago, they were home to some of history's most sophisticated cultures, including the Inca people, who mined the mountains for gold and carved massive cities into their sides. And the potato, high in nutrients and able to be farmed even in that unforgiving environment, was their fuel.

WHO ARE YOU CALLIN' A COUCH **POTATO?**

When Spanish sailors first brought potatoes across the Pacific Ocean in the 16th century, Europeans turned up their noses at the dirt brown lumps. They refused to eat them, using potatoes as decorative garden plants instead. When famine struck Prussia in 1744, King Frederick the Great had to order his peasants to eat spuds to keep from starving.

Over time, farmers started to realize that potato plants produced an astounding amount of food. Planting potato crops doubled Europe's food supply. Potatoes nourished a well-fed working class, allowing the British, Dutch, and German empires to become world powers. Their people went on to run the factories of the industrial revolution, which changed how people lived in much of the world. And it was all because of the humble spud.

Bet You Didn't Know

Potatoes are closely related to deadly nightshade (also called belladonna), a plant so toxic it was often used as a poison in the ancient world.

I DON'T LIKE FRY-DAYS!

CHILI PEPPERS

A **Hot** History

THE ORIGINAL **RED HOT CHILI PEPPERS!**

SPICE UP YOUR LIFE!

You're chowing down on a tasty taco when it hits you: a searing fire that burns your mouth and makes your eyes water. The culprit? A chili pepper.

Humans have been adding chilies to their meals for over 6,000 years. The peppers not only add a spicy kick, they also help keep food from spoiling—a huge bonus in the days before refrigeration. The Aztec of central Mexico even used chilies as medicine, writing that the potent plant could cure toothaches. They were right—the chemical that gives chilies their kick, capsaicin, can trigger the body to block pain signals.

Chilies are native to only one area of the world: the Americas. By the time Columbus arrived in the late 15th century, chilies were an essential food there. Columbus had been looking for a new sea route for spices grown in Asia—most importantly, black pepper. Instead, he sailed home with a different pepper: the chili.

Easy and inexpensive to grow, chili peppers were a flavoring the masses could afford. Within 50 years of their arrival in Spain, they had spread across much of Asia and into West Africa, North Africa, the Middle East, Italy, and Eastern Europe. Today, we consider them an essential part of the cuisines of these places—like Indian curries and Hungarian goulash. Imagine how different those dishes would taste without the spread of the fiery chili across the world!

GHOST PEPPERS WHO?

Bet You **Didn't Know**

Birds can't taste chili spice.

119

A **Culinary** ADVENTURE!

Every day, people across the world munch on a variety of awesome foods. Depending on where you grew up, some of these foods might seem surprising, but the truth is, many of them are incredibly nutritious—and beyond simply expanding your palate, eating some of them can be good for the planet! See what lip-smacking delicious delicacies people dine on around the globe.

Insects

In many parts of the world, insects are considered a delicacy. People in the Oaxaca region of Mexico stuff fried grasshoppers into tacos. In Cambodia, tarantulas are dipped in batter and fried into doughnuts. In Southeast Asia, locusts and scorpions are sometimes served on skewers. An added bonus? Insects have an exceptionally high nutritional value compared to other protein sources, and they don't require many resources to thrive, which makes them a very sustainable snack!

YOUR
DAILY
PROTEIN!

Ancient Eggs

A traditional Chinese dish, 1,000-year-old eggs aren't really that old ... but they've still been preserved for as long as a few months. To make them, a hole is dug in the ground and a mixture of clay or ash, salt, lime, rice husks, tea, and straw is poured in. Then fresh duck, quail, or chicken eggs are buried in it. As the eggs gradually absorb the mixture, their yolks turn dark green and the whites turn brown.

WELL WE'RE NOT **EGG-XACTLY** ANCIENT.

Jellied Moose Nose

In the cold climates of Canada and Alaska, U.S.A., moose is often used in ways that people in other regions might eat beef: as steaks and sausages, for example. Indigenous people traditionally used every part of the animal—from feet to nose. After a long simmer in broth, the meat is placed in a loaf pan and chilled until it forms a jelly.

Seaweed

Many cultures have enjoyed these ocean plants for centuries. In Japan, 20 species of seaweed are used in common dishes. Koreans often celebrate birthdays with seaweed soup. And long ago, seaweed was a traditional ingredient in Scotland and Ireland. Today, it's enjoying growing popularity around the world as a snack food.

WHO ARE YOU CALLING **A WEED?**

MEATBALLS

Globs of the **Globe**

I'M A CITIZEN OF THE **WORLD.**

Bet You **Didn't Know**

Marinara sauce got its name because the wives of sailors, or mariners, would stir together a quick mix of garlic, oil, and tomatoes when they spotted their husbands' returning fishing boats in the distance, so they could have dinner waiting for them when they got home.

Round and plump, swimming in red sauce and plopped atop a pile of spaghetti—there's nothing more Italian than classic meatballs, right? Wrong.

The meatballs familiar to most Americans are large in size and contain moist bread crumbs, herbs, cheese, egg, and a mix of meats such as beef and pork or veal. They're doused in marinara sauce and served on a bowl of spaghetti. But they are nothing like traditional Italian meatballs, called *polpette*. These can be as small as marbles, are made of various meats from turkey to fish, and are almost always served in a light broth instead of tomato sauce. And they're never paired with spaghetti.

The meatball many of us know today was a creation of Italian-American immigrants in the late 19th and early 20th centuries. Most had very little money, so they had to make the polpette of their home countries with the cheapest cuts of meat available.

To boost the flavor factor, they added marinara sauce. And to make a full meal out of a little meat, they added lots of bread crumbs to their meatballs and served them with spaghetti. As the immigrants grew more prosperous, their meatballs grew, too, becoming larger and made with choicer cuts and less bread.

But far from being American or Italian, meatballs are a food of the world. The Vietnamese eat *bò viên* in bowls of soup, and the Swedish enjoy *köttbullar* in thick brown gravy. The Spanish have *albondigas* and the South Africans *skilpadjies*. Meatballs for everyone!

TACOS

That's a **Wrap**

MAKE EVERY DAY **TACO TUESDAY.**

In a single year, more than 4.5 billion tacos are consumed in America alone—that's enough to stretch to the moon and back! From tiny street tacos to fast-food versions dripping with yellow cheese, tacos in all forms are beloved.

Some experts think the word "taco" originated in Mexican silver mines of the 18th century. Then, "taco" referred to slips of paper miners would wrap around gunpowder to blow holes in the earth in their search for shiny metal. Later, the word came to represent the tortilla-wrapped food that resembled the explosive.

Tacos became a favorite food of the working class across Mexico. Different regions are still famous today for their unique variations, such as fried fish tacos from the Pacific coast and pork carnitas tacos from the state of Michoacán in central Mexico. In the late 19th and early 20th centuries, when Mexican migrants came to the United States to work in mines and on railroads, they brought tacos with them.

Meanwhile, Mexican cooks borrowed taco ideas from other cultures: Lebanese migrants to Mexico brought shawarma, lamb cooked on vertical rotisseries. The usual pork was swapped for lamb, a dash of pineapple was added, and *tacos al pastor* became a standard Mexican dish. (*Pastor* means "shepherd," the local name for the Lebanese merchants who introduced the idea.) Today, you can find tacos everywhere from fancy restaurants to fast-food drive-throughs.

TACO 'BOUT A FAN FAVORITE!

Bet You **Didn't Know**

The largest taco in the world included 1,183 pounds (537 kg) of grilled steak, 186 pounds (85 kg) of dough, 179 pounds (81 kg) of onion, and 106 pounds (48 kg) of cilantro. It took six hours to make.

SOY
SAUCE

One **Boss Sauce**

I HAVE BEEN AROUND THE **(TOFU)** BLOCK!

Salty, tangy, and pungent, soy sauce is an ingredient and condiment enjoyed all over the globe. But how did a liquid made from fermented soybeans take over the world?

Thousands of years ago, when there were no refrigerators to keep food fresh, people had to find creative ways to preserve their meat so they could survive through the winter. Like many others around the world, the people of China used salt: Their method was to pack their meat in the stuff. They discovered that in the process, the salt added tasty flavors to the preserved food.

At least 2,000 years ago, the Chinese started making these preserved foods into thick pastes known as *jiang*. All kinds of

meats, fish, vegetables, and grains were used to make different kinds of jiang. But of all these ingredients, soybeans were easiest to grow. By the time of the Han dynasty from 206 B.C. to A.D. 220, they had become jiang's primary ingredient.

Eventually, jiang made from soybeans became a sauce in its own right, made by straining the flavorful liquid from soybeans fermented in salty brine. By the late 18th century, it was the most important seasoning in Chinese cuisine. Not long after, it was an essential part of the dishes of Japan, Korea, and Southeast Asia. Today, it's slurped up nearly everywhere: In the United States, soy sauce is the third most popular condiment behind mayonnaise and ketchup.

THIRD ... **FOR NOW!**

Bet You **Didn't Know**

Traditional soy sauce is thicker, sweeter, and less salty than the version known to most Westerners.

CHAPTER 6

Traditions

Have you ever wondered why an oversize rabbit brings eggs on Easter? Or why we like to scare ourselves silly in haunted houses at Halloween? Many modern holidays and traditions have roots that stretch far back in time—sometimes thousands of years. And those prehistoric customs were often nothing like the ones we celebrate today.

I AM SUCH AN **ICON!**

FLAGS

Flying **High**

We salute them, fly them as a symbol of respect, and wave them to show our pride. But did you know flags were originally tools of war?

Thousands of years before modern flags, armies from ancient Egypt, Persia, and Babylonia carried long poles topped with animal figures. Soldiers believed these totems would help them channel the spiritual power of the creature during battle. But they were also practical: Hoisted high above the ground, they were rallying points that signaled where fighters should regroup during combat. The influence of these flag ancestors can still be seen on modern flagpoles, which are often topped with creatures such as eagles.

At least 3,000 years ago, Chinese production of silk allowed them to fly the first fabric banners, often adorned with red birds, white tigers, or blue dragons. Soldiers relied on flags during battle as a way to find their own troops. Soon enough, opposing armies realized that the fall of a flag would confuse the enemy. Soldiers began to target flags as the first point of attack.

During the Middle Ages, nobles protected their kingdoms with elite soldiers called knights. Since their faces were often covered by armor, they used flags as a way to identify themselves and their positions while fighting. As the age of exploration began and European ships set forth to conquer other lands, they used flags to announce their country of origin and military status from a distance. Victors of sea battles began to tear down the enemy's flag and replace it with their own, symbolizing their military might. Today, we still rally behind flags as markers of unity and victory.

Bet You **Didn't Know**

Since flags have to look the same on both sides, most don't show words.

PRAYER FLAGS ALONG THE ROUTE TO MOUNT EVEREST

EASTER
An Egg-cellent Tale

Every Easter, many kids excitedly await the arrival of a giant egg-toting bunny. It's one of the oldest and most important Christian holidays, celebrating the resurrection of Jesus Christ from the dead. But the origins of Easter date to long before Christianity existed.

SOMETHING'S OFF!

Since prehistoric times, people have celebrated the spring equinox, when the amount of daylight and darkness are exactly the same length. It signaled that the long winter was coming to a close—a big deal in a time when many people didn't survive the season. The word "Easter" comes from the pagan goddess Eostre, who was worshipped long ago in Anglo-Saxon England. The goddess was often depicted as a rabbit, an animal that symbolizes birth and renewal because it's known for having big families.

Eggs are another tradition dating back to long ago. For ancient Egyptians, eggs were a representation of the sun, which is reborn every morning. They, along with the ancient Persians, would color and eat eggs during their spring festivals to celebrate the birth of the new season.

Around the 13th century, Christian leaders prohibited eating eggs in the week before Easter (known as Holy Week). But the chickens continued to lay. People started decorating those excess eggs to identify their holy status and, over time, Easter eggs came to symbolize Jesus' rebirth after death.

Bet You **Didn't Know**

Not every culture has an Easter bunny. In Australia, where rabbits are considered pests, a marsupial called a bilby hands out gifts. Norwegians celebrate Easter with chickens, and the French with church bells.

HAUNTED
HOUSES

A **Spooky** Story

Boo! In this frightfully fun chamber of horrors, zombies shuffle forward and ghouls lurk in corners, ready to pop out at unsuspecting victims. Haunted houses are part of many people's traditional Halloween celebrations. But where did this terrifying tradition come from?

The first haunted house was the creation of a clever entrepreneur named Marie Tussaud. In 1802, she opened a ghastly exhibition in London: wax sculptures of people who had been decapitated by the guillotine during the French Revolution, including Marie Antoinette and King Louis XVI. Tussaud's depictions were incredibly lifelike because to make them she used plaster casts, called death masks, made from the actual faces of her subjects. British audiences were frightened and delighted, and Tussaud's "Chamber of Horrors" remained in business until 2016.

During the early 1900s, American parents were looking for a way to keep their teenagers out of trouble on Halloween. They started decorating their basements with spiderwebs and black cats and inviting the local kids to go house to house for a thrilling scare. Walt Disney commercialized the idea when he opened Disneyland's Haunted Mansion in 1969. More than 80,000 people braved the horrors within a single day. Disney's Haunted Mansion sparked a spooky trend, and soon haunted houses were popping up across the country. Today, more than 2,500 of them scare the daylights out of people every Halloween.

BOO!

A WAX FIGURE OF MARIE TUSSAUD

DEMONS, YOU SAY? HAVEN'T SEEN ANY.

Bet You Didn't Know

The Halloween tradition of wearing scary costumes comes from the ancient Celts, who believed dressing up as demons would confuse spirits from the underworld who roamed the streets during Halloween.

FRIGHTFUL
Fairy Tales

Magical happenings, frolicking woodland creatures, and, of course, Prince Charming—fairy tales might seem like sweet stories. But the tales we've been told since childhood often have unexpectedly gruesome origins.

GIVE A
LITTLE
WHISTLE!

Pinocchio

The wooden puppet we know today is a little naughty—after all, his nose grows every time he lies. But the original Pinocchio was downright bad. After he's carved, he runs away from his foster father, Geppetto, then tricks the police into putting Geppetto in jail. When his conscience—in the form of a talking cricket—makes him feel guilty, Pinocchio simply squashes the insect.

SEE? I'M NOT THE ONLY **BADDIE** HERE!

Snow White

In both the original and the modern tale, Snow White has to fend off the Evil Queen's murder attempts at every turn. But in some early versions, Snow White doesn't just live happily ever after—she gets revenge. When the Evil Queen attends her wedding, Snow White forces a pair of burning-hot iron shoes on the queen's feet and makes her dance until she collapses.

The Little Mermaid

OUCH!

DR. SCHOLL'S CAN'T SAVE ME NOW!

As the modern story goes, the little mermaid falls for a handsome—but landlocked—prince, and trades her fins for legs to be with him. This version left out some original details: For example, the mermaid's new legs come with a curse that makes her feel like she's walking on knives with each step.

Cinderella

In today's version, the evil stepmother is disappointed when the glass slipper doesn't fit on her daughters' feet, but she gets over it. Not so much in the earlier takes on the tale. One has the stepmother so determined to squeeze the daughters' feet into the slipper that she cuts them down to size.

137

GROUNDHOG DAY

Winter **Predictor**

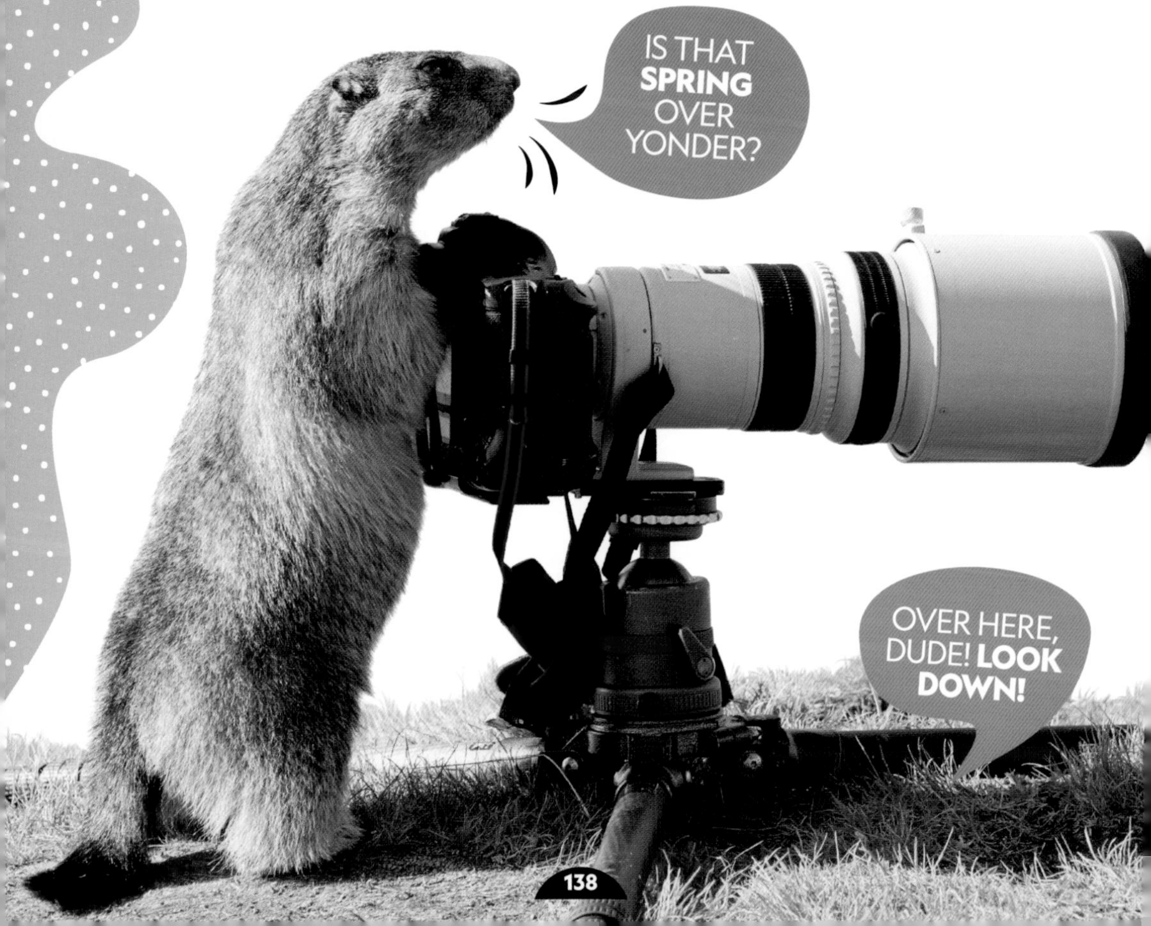

Every year on February 2 in Punxsutawney, Pennsylvania, U.S.A., tens of thousands of people gather to watch a groundhog predict the weather. If the rodent meteorologist sees his shadow, that means six more weeks of winter. If he doesn't, an early spring is on its way. How did this bizarre ritual get started?

The ancient Celts celebrated February 2 as a holy day marking the beginning of spring. As Christianity spread through Europe, the pagan tradition evolved into a religious feast called Candlemas. In certain areas, people believed that a sunny Candlemas predicted 40 more days of chilly weather. In Germany, the day only counted as sunny if badgers and other small animals saw their shadows.

When German immigrants settled in Pennsylvania beginning in the 18th century, they brought their custom with them. Instead of the badger, they chose the native groundhog as their Candlemas animal. Groundhogs—also called woodchucks—hibernate the winter away in underground burrows. In February, male groundhogs wake up and come to the surface to look for a mate before returning to hibernation until March.

Bet You **Didn't Know**

Instead of Groundhog Day, Texas celebrates "Armadillo Day." Bee Cave Bob the armadillo predicts both the weather and, in election years, the next president of the United States.

In 1887, the first official Groundhog Day took place when the people of Punxsutawney trekked to a hilltop called Gobbler's Knob to witness the weather-forecasting powers of the groundhog. The first "Punxsutawney Phil" saw his shadow, kicking off one of America's stranger celebrations. It's stuck around for more than a century— even though Phil is only right about 40 percent of the time.

PUNXSUTAWNEY PHIL

PARADES

Something to **Celebrate**

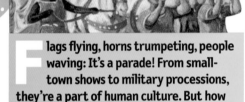

Flags flying, horns trumpeting, people waving: It's a parade! From small-town shows to military processions, they're a part of human culture. But how did they get started?

Parades were born on the battlefield. As far back as ancient Mesopotamia, rulers would decorate buildings with images that showed off their position of authority, often depicting themselves at the head of their armies. In ancient Rome, victorious emperors would march to Rome's Temple of Jupiter, with toga-wearing senators and ranks of soldiers following.

As history marched on, parades became a way for militaries to show off their power to the people. Prussia, once a German state with origins in the 16th century, became famous for the precision of its military processions. Armies around the world followed Prussia's lead, with salutes and drills showing off their skills and discipline.

Over time, a different kind of parade stepped up, too: one that was just for fun. In the 1840s, traveling circuses would parade through town to attract business, complete with clowns to entertain the audience. In the early 19th century, throwing candy became part of the tradition when parade participants tossed treats to the crowd during a Mardi Gras parade in New Orleans, Louisiana, U.S.A. One of the most famous modern parades is the Macy's Thanksgiving Day Parade in New York City, which showcases giant balloons shaped like dinosaurs, superheroes, and cartoon characters.

Bet You **Didn't Know**

A single Macy's parade float can use 200 pounds (91 kg) of glitter.

TRICKED YA!

MASSKARA FESTIVAL, BACOLOD CITY, PHILIPPINES

NEW YEAR'S

Big Beginnings

YOU
ARE MY
**NUMBER
ONE!**

A FATHER GIVING
OTOSHIDAMA
(A NEW YEAR'S
GIFT OF MONEY)
TO HIS DAUGHTER

All around the world, people ring in the new year with countdowns, kisses, and fireworks. People have been welcoming the new year for more than 4,000 years—but their parties looked very different from modern ones.

¡FELIZ AÑO NUEVO!

Historians think the earliest New Year's celebration happened in Mesopotamia (modern-day Iraq and other nearby countries) around 2000 B.C. The Mesopotamians went all out, marking the holiday with an 11-day festival called Akitu. During this time, the king's rule was renewed. To see if he was worthy, he went through a ritual in which he was dragged around by his ears to see if he would cry. If he did, it was a sign that the gods were satisfied and he was free to rule for another year.

Different cultures celebrated the New Year at different times: The Babylonians chose the spring equinox; the ancient Egyptians marked it when the Nile River flooded its banks. That changed when Roman dictator Julius Caesar came to power. He created a new calendar and named it after himself, the Julian calendar. It began the new year on January 1 to honor Janus, a Roman god whose two faces allowed him to look back into the past and forward into the future.

Today, many (but not all) cultures celebrate New Year's Day on January 1, but different countries still retain their own traditions. In Spain, people eat a dozen grapes just before midnight in honor of the 12 upcoming months. In Mexico, ring-shaped pastries show that the year has come full circle. And in many places, people make resolutions, a tradition that dates all the way back to the ancient Mesopotamians, who made promises to their gods that they would do better in the coming year.

Bet You **Didn't Know**

One famous New Year's tradition is the dropping of a giant ball at midnight in New York City's Times Square. In other places in the United States, people drop other items: pickles in Dillsburg, Pennsylvania, and possums in Tallapoosa, Georgia.

Manners
AROUND THE WORLD

Hey, world traveler! Want to feel right at home as you eat your way across the globe? Here are some things to know about different cultures' customs that will keep you in the good graces of your local hosts.

IN FRANCE:
Don't Put Bread on Your Plate

Etiquette is *trés* important to the French. There, bread should be placed on the table, never on your plate. And it's not an appetizer—use it to wipe up the last delicious traces of your meal.

IN TAIWAN:
Belch After Eating

In Taiwan, China, and some other Asian countries, belching is considered a sign that you've enjoyed your meal. Compliments to the chef!

BURRRRP!

IN CHILE:
Never Eat With Your Hands

Grabbing food with your fingers is seen as truly vulgar in Chile. Chileans consider it polite to eat everything with utensils—including foods some might consider finger foods, like french fries!

EH, NO HANDS!

STAY AWAY, YOU **MONSTER!**

THIS **DOESN'T** SEEM GOOD …

IN NEW YORK CITY: Never Eat Pizza With a Fork

When enjoying the Big Apple's most famous food, visitors sometimes reach for a utensil instead of picking up their piping-hot slice with their hands. But New Yorkers consider this a major faux pas. (Or should we say "dough" pas?)

IN ITALY: Don't Pass the Cheese

Italians take their food seriously. You should never ask for cheese unless it's been offered, and it's considered particularly bad manners if you add cheese to a seafood pasta dish.

IN JAPAN: Be Careful With Your Chopsticks

It's considered impolite to cross them or lick them, but most important, don't ever stick your chopsticks upright in a bowl of rice. In Japan, that's a practice done only at funerals, when the rice bowl of the deceased is placed before the coffin, with chopsticks stuck vertically in the rice.

THE **CHINESE** ZODIAC

What's Your **Sign?**

Are you a rat? Or perhaps you're an ox? A tiger, or even a dragon? These animals represent signs in the Chinese zodiac. The zodiac is a system of 12 animal signs that repeat in a 12-year cycle. Tradition says the animal assigned to your birth year reveals secrets about your personality, future career, and luck in love.

The different animals are said to bring different personality traits to the people born in that year. Rats, for example, are natural leaders. Oxen are hardworking, but they can be stubborn. Tigers are brave, and dragons are highly creative. Does your sign match your personality?

According to legend, the Chinese zodiac began when an emperor commanded all the animals in the universe to compete in a race. Twelve creatures, including the rabbit, the snake, and the horse, answered the call. As they competed, they revealed their true traits: The rat won the race, but only by jumping on the back of the ox. The dragon would have come in first, but it stopped to help people caught in a flood.

What's the real story? Experts aren't sure, but some think the creatures of the zodiac origi-nated with the animals that ancient nomadic tribes used to hunt. Over time, 12 different animals came to represent each year in the cycle.

THANKS, BUD!

Bet You **Didn't Know**

According to one folktale, there's no cat in the Chinese zodiac because the cat over-slept when the animals were being chosen.

MISTLETOE

Plant a **Kiss**

Smooching under a sprig of mistletoe is a well-known holiday tradition. But mistletoe is far from sweet; it's actually a parasite that survives by stealing from other plants.

Mistletoe has roots shaped like spears that stab into the branches of larger trees and suck up their water and nutrients. There are hundreds of species of mistletoe that cling to trees and shrubs all over the world. Because mistletoe could blossom even during their frozen winters, the Celtic Druids of the first century B.C. thought it had magical powers. They used it to treat illnesses, to keep nightmares at bay, and even to predict the future.

The Norse believed that the plant was a sacred symbol of Frigga, the goddess of love. In one version of a myth, Loki, the god of mischief, shot Frigga's son with an arrow.

The gods brought him back to life under a mistletoe tree, and Frigga was so delighted she vowed to plant a kiss on everyone who stood beneath one.

The tradition was taken very seriously in Victorian England during the 19th century. Etiquette decreed that a gentleman should pluck a berry from the mistletoe branch before landing a smooch. The kisses could continue until the berries ran out. What the Victorians didn't know was that mistletoe berries contain a toxic substance that can cause vomiting. How romantic.

FRIGGA, NORSE GODDESS OF LOVE

PUCKER UP!

Bet You **Didn't Know**

The Victorians thought that refusing a kiss under the mistletoe brought bad luck.

DREIDELS

Topsy-Turvy Tale

Potato pancakes, jelly doughnuts, chocolate coins. The hanukkiah with its nine flickering candles. And of course, the spinning top called a dreidel. They're all traditions of Hanukkah, the eight-day Jewish "festival of lights." But how did a toy become part of the celebration?

Dreidels are used to play a game in which players collect or give up pieces depending on which side is facing up when the top stops spinning. But according to a popular legend, the game wasn't always just for fun: In ancient Greece, the Jewish people were forbidden from studying the holy scriptures called the Torah. Instead of giving up the Torah, Jewish scholars outsmarted the Greeks by spinning tops while practicing their studies. If they were spotted, it looked like they were just playing a game.

The modern dreidel probably originated in Ireland around the 16th century. Later, the top spun its way to Germany, where it acquired four letters that represent moves in the game: *N* (for the German word *Nichts*, or "nothing"), *G* (*Ganz*, or "all"), *H* (*Halb*, or "half"), and *S* (*Stell ein*, or "put in").

When the game was adopted by Germany's Jewish communities, they wrote the letters in Hebrew and assigned them new words: a Hebrew sentence meaning "a great miracle happened there," referring to the miracle of the lamp oil, which Hanukkah commemorates. (The oil should have lasted one day but ended up lasting eight days.) After that, the dreidel whirled its way to Hanukkah celebrations around the world.

Bet You **Didn't Know**

In New York City, participants in the Major League Dreidel tournament send their tops turning on a surface called the "Spinagogue" to see whose can go the longest.

EYES ON THE **PRIZE!**

CHAPTER 7

Athletics & Activities

Swooshing down snowy hillsides on skis, spinning ourselves silly on carnival rides—some activities are just for fun ... or are they? Read on to learn how the first films caused audiences to panic and how the sport of skiing was once used as a battle tactic. One thing is for sure: These histories are more than mere entertainment.

PICNICS

Outside Eats

SUMMER-
TIME
PARTY!

LUNCH IS
HERE, **BOYS!**

Prehistoric man probably didn't yearn to dine outdoors. After all, every meal was a picnic back then. After people moved indoors for mealtimes, meals eaten outside were no longer a necessity. But we never forgot about them.

One of the earliest descriptions of a picnic comes from tales of the legendary English hero Robin Hood. Ballads described the hero and his Merry Men passing around bread and cheese under the shade of trees in Sherwood Forest. Meals eaten outdoors probably became fashionable around the Middle Ages, when wealthy nobles would organize hunting parties in the woods that ended in an elaborate feast.

Until the Victorian Era, picnics remained a treat just for the wealthy. By that time, the industrial revolution had led farmers to hang up their hoes and move to cities to find work in factories. By 1850, half the population of England lived in urban areas. People began to pine for fresh country air and open fields.

Picnics became the height of fashion among middle-class Victorians. But unlike people today, they weren't scarfing down squashed PB&Js in brown paper bags. Picnicking Victorians brought tables, linens, crystal, chairs, and servants—along with gourmet food such as meat pies, roast chicken, and cheesecakes. Imagine packing up that picnic!

Bet You **Didn't Know**

Luxury car company Rolls-Royce makes an upscale picnic basket that sells for $46,000.

YOU WILL BE
STUFFED!

TILT-A-WHIRL

A **Spin** Through **History**

In this amusement park staple, cars attached to a rotating platform spin wildly in unpredictable directions. The Tilt-A-Whirl has become a classic ride. But where did it come from?

It all started with a woodworker in Faribault, Minnesota, U.S.A., named Herbert Sellner. After inventing an early version of the waterslide in 1923, Sellner was looking for a new idea for an amusement park ride—one that would keep people guessing about its next move. One day, while playing with his young son, Sellner placed him in a chair with wheels on top of the family's kitchen table, then shook and spun the table. (Don't try this at home!) When the boy giggled with delight, Sellner knew he had found his idea.

Sellner built 14 prototypes of the Tilt-A-Whirl in his basement and yard. Made out of wood, the original ride had nine spinning cars attached by a long arm to a central platform. As the cars moved, they would tilt, swing, snap from side to side, or spin unpredictably. By 1927, Sellner had opened his own manufacturing company and debuted his ride at the Minnesota State Fair. It was a hit.

Since then, Tilt-A-Whirls have come to be a classic ride at carnivals, fairs, and amusement parks. Take a spin on one and you'll be one of more than 70 million people who ride a Tilt-A-Whirl each year. Just be careful not to lose your lunch!

Bet You **Didn't Know**

Because the motion of a Tilt-A-Whirl depends on the weight and position of its riders, no two rides are ever the same.

SELLNER'S PROTOTYPE

FILMS

AAAND …
ACTION!

The earliest films astounded and amazed audiences. Glimpses of girl gunslinger Annie Oakley in action or prizefighters duking it out in the ring transported people to an event that they never would have been able to watch in person.

Compared to the movies of today, the first films were extremely primitive. Nevertheless, they astounded people who had never seen such a thing before. One early film featured a shot of a train pulling into a station, headed directly for the camera. One cinema myth that has since been debunked is that the sight of the train coming head-on scared viewers so badly that some in the front rows panicked and ran out!

At first, movies were meant for only one person, who watched through a peephole viewer window on a device called the Kinetoscope. The films were collections of scenes, such as a man watering his garden or a street vendor selling his wares. One of the first movies to tell a story, 1903's *The Great Train Robbery*, showed a heist in a silent but action-packed 12 minutes.

Filmmakers wanted to make longer, more complex movies, but they faced off against production companies that wanted to save money by continuing to use the cameras and viewers that were built for short movies. So many aspiring moviemakers left the eastern United States, where film was born, and moved to a place with enough sunshine for them to film outside most of the year—Hollywood, in Los Angeles, California.

Bet You **Didn't Know**

The names of actors in early movies were not released, because producers feared they might become famous and demand more money.

TRAIN-ING FOR MY SCREEN DEBUT!

MOVIE **Magic**

A car speeds across a crumbling bridge, seconds away from a fatal fall into the water below. Just before the last piece of pavement disintegrates—*vroom!*—the vehicle is airborne, impossibly arcing through the sky to land on solid ground. Today, we're used to special effects like these. But they were more than a century in the making.

Movie Monsters

Filmmakers have been using plaster, wood, and papier-mâché to create fantastical characters since the early 1900s. But the technique was taken to new heights in 1993's *Jurassic Park*. Computer graphics were combined with mechanically controlled puppet dinosaurs, including a 20-foot (6-m) *T. rex*.

Delightful Dino

Performer Winsor McCay needed something to wow audiences in 1914. So he used more than 10,000 drawings to create *Gertie the Dinosaur*, the first animation to feature a character with a distinct personality. McCay, performing onstage, would give Gertie a series of commands, and she would respond on the screen.

Miniature Worlds

French illusionist and film director Georges Méliès pioneered the technique of using miniature models to create special effects. His 1902 film *A Trip to the Moon* showed a model rocket crashing into the face of an actor wearing moon makeup. Miniatures are still around today: In the Lord of the Rings trilogy, director Peter Jackson used them to create the scenery of Middle-earth.

Brought to Life

Toy Story, the first full-length computer-generated film ever, hit theaters in 1995. Twenty-seven animators, part of a team of 110 who worked on the film, spent four years bringing the movie to life. It took 800,000 hours just to edit. But all that work paid off: *Toy Story* made more than $361 million. And it changed animated moviemaking forever.

Wealth of Water

The record for priciest special effect in history goes to 1956's *The Ten Commandments*. To bring one of the Bible's greatest miracles—the parting of the Red Sea—to life, director Cecil B. DeMille filmed 300,000 gallons (1.1 million L) of water being poured into a massive tank, then played the shot backward.

Motion Tricks

1963's *Jason and the Argonauts* shows an army of skeletons rising from the ground for a fight between the living and the dead. The scene was one of the most famous early uses of the stop-motion technique, in which puppets or models are pains-takingly moved and photo-graphed one frame at a time.

161

SKIING

A **Sport** on the **Edge**

Swish! Today, we think of skiing as a sport, involving racing down a snowy mountain at thrilling speeds. But for most of its history, skiing was a useful way to get from place to place—such a good mode of transportation, in fact, that it was even used in battle!

Skiing has been around for so long that the ski was invented before the wheel. Some 22,000-year-old cave drawings hint that prehistoric people may have made primitive skis by attaching sticks to their feet during the last ice age, when Earth was much colder and snowier than it is now. Skis would have enabled early humans to cross wetlands and marshes in the winter when they froze over, and to track reindeer and elk across the frozen tundra.

A skier's ability to travel quickly and quietly across vast distances made skis an ideal tool for the military. As long ago as A.D. 1200, the Norse deployed troops on skis to battle Vikings. In 1939, during World War II, a small force of Finnish ski troops managed to hold off an invading Soviet army three times its size. Wearing white uniforms that camouflaged them in the snow, the ski-mounted Fins zipped in and out of the forest, tossing explosives inside Soviet tanks.

Meanwhile, skiing had also evolved into a sport. In the 1760s, the Norwegian army held competitions in skiing down slopes, around trees, and across snowy fields while shooting at targets. These early races would later become Olympic events.

WANT TO SEE ME DO A **HALF-PIPE?**

Bet You **Didn't Know**

Italian skier Simone Origone (shown) once held the world record for the fastest downhill ski speed—but his brother, Ivan Origone, beat his record in 2016, with a speed of 158.4 miles an hour (255 km/h)!

WRESTLING

Storied Smackdown

Grappling with another human until one fighter admits defeat might not be everyone's idea of fun. But wrestling is the oldest form of recreational combat, something humans have been fascinated with since the beginning of civilization.

Carvings and drawings from between 15,000 and 20,000 years ago found in caves in southern Europe appear to depict the sport. Egyptian wall paintings from around 3400 B.C. show wrestlers in holds still used today. And there is evidence that the Mesopotamians and ancient Chinese wrestled, too. But it was the ancient Greeks who elevated it from sport to art form.

The ancient Greeks held wrestling in such high esteem that it was the final and most important discipline in the five-sport pentathlon. After the discus, the javelin, the long jump, and the foot race, athletes wrestled. They competed naked, their bodies coated with slippery olive oil, then covered with a thin layer of sand to protect them from the summer sunlight or the winter's chill.

Today's World Wrestling Entertainment (WWE) wrestlers are often seen whacking each other over the heads with folding chairs or diving into a body slam from the top of the ropes. These matches aren't so much sports as they are choreographed spectacles. It turns out wrestling matches have been fixed since the time of ancient Rome. A papyrus dating to A.D. 267 outlines a contract in which a teenage wrestler named Demetrius agreed to throw the match for 3,800 drachmas— about the cost of a donkey.

Bet You **Didn't Know**

The ancient Greek sport of *pankration* combined elements of wrestling and boxing in a competition so fierce that only biting and gouging out the opponent's eyes were forbidden.

GOLF

Whack-a-Ball

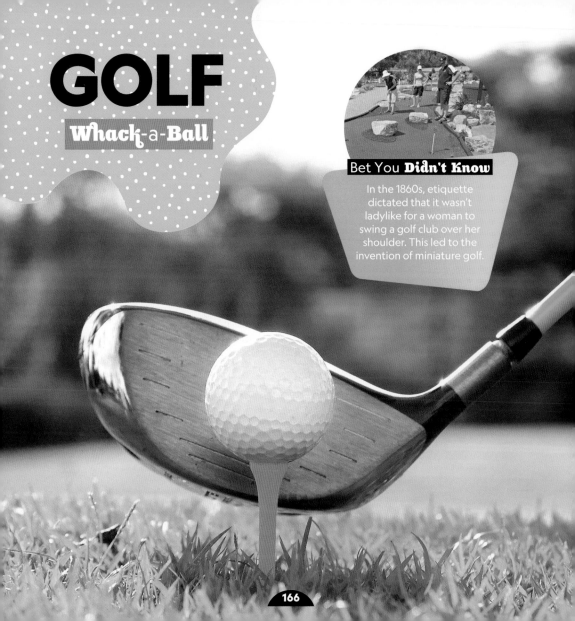

If you think about it, the sport of golf seems like it's setting the participants up for failure: Hit a tiny ball over and over until it makes it past sand pits, trees, and ponds, and all the way into a little hole off in the distance. Repeat 18 times. Nevertheless, people have been obsessed with golf for a very long time.

PUT YOUR BEST FOOT **FORE**-WARD?

MARY STUART, QUEEN OF SCOTS

Many cultures claim to have invented the sport. The ancient Romans played a golflike game called *paganica* using a bent stick and a leather ball stuffed with feathers. The Belgians had *chole*, in which players tried to hit targets with the fewest strokes. And in the Netherlands, people played a similar game called *kolven* or *kolf* in a court with walls.

The true game of golf came to be around the 15th century A.D., on the wide-open lands of Scotland. Players became so obsessed with the idea of hitting a ball into a faraway hole that in 1457 King James II complained that the sport was interfering with his soldiers' archery practice. A few decades later, King James IV even tried to ban the game—but he later gave up the effort and started playing himself.

In 1565, Mary Queen of Scots became the first known female golfer; she was criticized by the church for playing just days after her husband was murdered. She later helped spread the sport to France when she traveled there to study. The term "caddy," the assistant who carries a golfer's clubs and gives playing advice, comes from the members of the French military who acted as the queen's helpers, known as cadets.

SWIFT Steeds

It would be hard to find an animal that has had more impact on human history than the horse. Horses could carry people and their cargo vast distances, and taming them allowed people to travel fast and far for the first time ever.

680 B.C.
Olympic Debut

Horses made their debut at the Olympic Games in ancient Greece pulling two-wheeled chariots around a track with hairpin turns at each end. It was one of the most exciting—and dangerous—events of the games.

500 B.C.
Post Service

Messengers mounted on horseback could carry messages 1,700 miles (2,736 km) in only seven days across the Persian Empire's Royal Road—a big improvement over the 90 days it took on foot.

3700 B.C.
The First Rider

3700 B.C.   1000 B.C.   500 B.C.   A.D. 1

At least 100,000 years ago, ancient humans hunted horses across the Eurasian steppes. It wasn't until about 6,000 years ago that one of them got the idea to climb up for a ride.

200 B.C.
Hands-Free

The invention of stirrups in China allowed riders to use their hands to throw spears, swing swords, or fire arrows while firmly in the saddle, and horses became a tool of war.

1700
North America
The indigenous people of North America adopted horses into their culture. They become experts at hunting from horseback.

Horses remained an important part of battle until the end of World War II, when they were phased out in favor of machines like the tank.

1945
On the Front Lines

500

1000

1500

2000

A.D. **700**
Knights
It took centuries for stirrups to reach Europe. When they did, they allowed warriors armored in heavy metal plates to mount, ride, and fight—the first knights.

SAFETY COMES **FIRST!**

ARCHERY

Aiming **High**

Today, archery is a sport. But for thousands of years, the bow and arrow was humankind's most lethal weapon. Archery is one of the most ancient arts still practiced today.

The earliest arrows were wooden sticks with stone heads, hurled at hungry predators about 50,000 years ago in North Africa. Fast-forward to 15,000 B.C. and the invention of the bow meant prehistoric people could fling projectiles at speeds that had never before been achieved. The new weapon allowed them to become better hunters. Archery brought early people greater safety, more food, and materials such as bone and hide. These helped ancient humans migrate while adapting to different environments.

Different cultures developed their own special sets of archery skills. During the Shang dynasty in China from 1766 to 1027 B.C.,

THAT'S A
BULL'S-EYE!

The ancient Egyptian pharaoh Tutankhamun was buried with bows and hundreds of arrows.

KNOWN WORLD, YOU'RE MINE!

GENGHIS KHAN

war chariots carried three-man teams that included an archer. The horse-riding Parthians, who lived in ancient Iran and Iraq from 247 B.C. to A.D. 224, could turn around in the saddle at high speeds and shoot attackers behind them. Around A.D. 1200, Mongolian ruler Genghis Khan used the bow and arrow to conquer much of the known world.

The bow and arrow remained the major tool of war until the 16th century, when it was mostly overtaken by firearms. But archery hung around as a sport, with English soldiers competing to hit a paper target on a mound of dirt up to 414 feet (126 m) away.

171

FERRIS WHEEL

Sky-High **Spinner**

When the county fair comes to town, you can count on fried food, impossible-to-win games, and, towering over it all, a giant spinning Ferris wheel. How did it get there?

In late 1890, architect Daniel Burnham was faced with a big challenge: how to turn a swampy square mile of Chicago into something people would flock from far and wide to see. Burnham decided that what his 1893 Chicago World's Fair really needed was a landmark so stunning it would rival the Eiffel Tower in Paris, France. The winning design came from an engineer named George Washington Gale Ferris, Jr.: a 250-foot (76-m)-wide revolving steel wheel with 36 cars seating 60 people each. It would carry adventurous fairgoers 25 stories into the air.

THE FLATIRON BUILDING IN NEW YORK CITY WAS DESIGNED BY DANIEL BURNHAM.

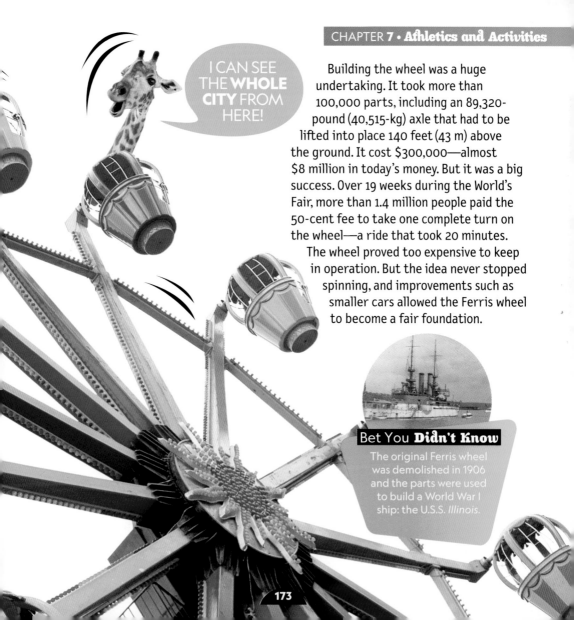

I CAN SEE THE **WHOLE CITY** FROM HERE!

Building the wheel was a huge undertaking. It took more than 100,000 parts, including an 89,320-pound (40,515-kg) axle that had to be lifted into place 140 feet (43 m) above the ground. It cost $300,000—almost $8 million in today's money. But it was a big success. Over 19 weeks during the World's Fair, more than 1.4 million people paid the 50-cent fee to take one complete turn on the wheel—a ride that took 20 minutes.

The wheel proved too expensive to keep in operation. But the idea never stopped spinning, and improvements such as smaller cars allowed the Ferris wheel to become a fair foundation.

Bet You **Didn't Know**

The original Ferris wheel was demolished in 1906 and the parts were used to build a World War I ship: the U.S.S. *Illinois*.

STARTING
BLOCKS

A **Race** Is **Afoot**

I FEEL THE NEED—THE NEED FOR **SPEED!**

On your mark, get set, go! During a race, like at the Olympics, or maybe at your school's track competitions, you might see runners line up and place their fingertips on the ground and set their feet on angled blocks. These blocks are called starting blocks. But how did *they* get their start?

The first footraces were run in ancient Greece, home of the original Olympics. As the Greeks perfected the sport, they came up with all kinds of methods to keep runners from taking off early and ruining the spectacle. One ancient jar discovered in Athens depicts runners at the start of a race with two horizontal cords connected to two posts acting as a barrier. At the start of the race, officials used a system of ropes to lower the barrier and begin the race. The design of early starting gates may have been inspired by the catapult, which used similar materials and design and was developed in the same place around the same time. Starting gates didn't turn into starting blocks until 1887. Then, Aboriginal sprinter Bobby McDonald shocked the crowd when he moved into a crouching position to start a race in Sydney, Australia. Soon, other runners took up the stance, which allows athletes to start the race with a surge of forward energy that can give them an advantage. To keep from slipping, track stars dug holes for their toes in the dirt until 1927, when the first modern, portable starting block was patented. The race was on.

Bet You **Didn't Know**

Because sound waves take time to travel to human ears, the average athlete takes at least one-tenth of a second to respond to a race's start signal.

CHAPTER 8

Ancient Inventions

You might not use an hourglass to tell time or buckle on a suit of armor for gym class. But at one time, the inventions in this chapter were everyday items. Some have been replaced by new creations, and others are still going strong, but they all changed history in unexpected ways.

THE WHEEL

Get **Rolling**

Of course wheels move cars, bikes, and skateboards from place to place. But look closely and you'll see them everywhere: They help glide your drawers in and out and pull your window shades up and down, and they spin fans, fishing reels, and toys. Wheels are so basic to our world that it's strange they weren't created until around 3500 B.C., after humans had already thought up all kinds of important inventions, including sailboats, sewing needles, woven cloth, and even the flute.

The first true wheel was likely used for pottery, not transportation. Around 3500 B.C., in Mesopotamia, a flat disk made of hardened clay was spun horizontally on an axis. That allowed potters to form blobs of wet clay into evenly shaped bowls and jars. But it took about three centuries longer before someone figured out they could turn this device on its side and use it to move two-wheeled chariots pulled by horses or donkeys.

The tricky part about inventing the wheel, experts say, was not figuring out how to roll something circular along the ground. It was figuring out how to attach that rolling circle to a platform that remains still— like a chariot or car body. For

POTTER'S WHEEL

HOW DO YOU **STOP** THIS THING?!

178

that, ancient inventors needed an axle, or a rod that passes through the wheel. To chisel axles and wheels to fit together just right, they needed metal tools—which didn't become common until about 4000 B.C.

Experts think that the wheel was so difficult to invent that it probably only happened once, in one place. Surrounding civilizations copied the design so rapidly that experts aren't sure exactly where the first true wheel rolled out. One thing's for sure: The modern world wouldn't move the same way without it.

WHEEL POWER!

Bet You Didn't Know

Ancient North Americans invented wheeled toys such as ceramic dogs. But they didn't use wheels for transportation—probably because they had no large domesticated animals that could pull carts.

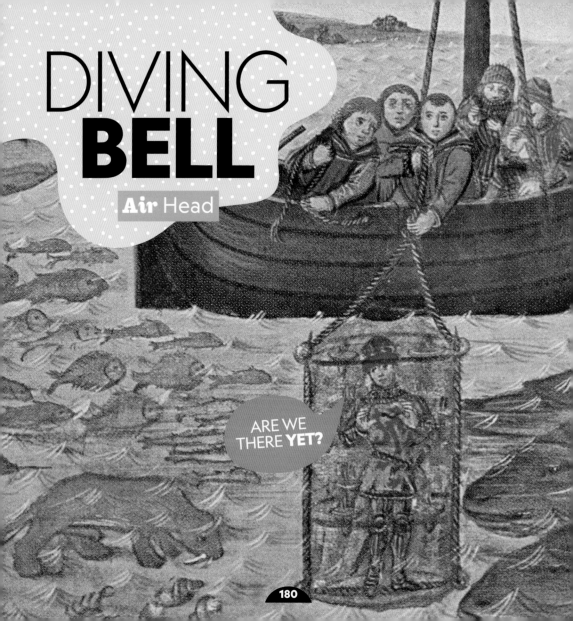

I AM A **TREASURE TROVE!**

For thousands of years, the area beneath the ocean's surface was a place humans could not go. The diving bell—an open-bottomed, air-filled chamber—led to the creation of something you're probably familiar with (the submarine!) and allowed humans to dive into a whole new world.

If you've ever held a cup upside down and pushed it underwater, you've noticed that the water's pressure holds the air inside. About 2,500 years ago, people realized that that they could breathe that trapped air.

They took large pots, stuck their heads in, and jumped into the nearest bodies of water. People could descend a dozen feet (3.7 m) or so, pop their heads out of these early diving bells, and take a quick look around before they ran out of air.

In 1588, the English navy defeated the Spanish Armada. Spanish prisoners of war spread the word that gold and treasures from their wrecked ships were spread all over the seafloor. Inventors rushed to outfit diving bells with systems of hoses and valves to replenish their oxygen. Divers could go deeper than ever before—but it was a risky business. They were more likely to burst their eardrums or suffocate to death than return to the surface with armfuls of riches.

In the late 1700s, workers used diving bells to fix the crumbling foundation of England's Hexham Bridge. But shortly after surfacing, some would mysteriously suffer strokes that led to paralysis and death. It took more than 100 years for scientists to work out that the problem was the pressure underwater, which caused tiny bubbles of nitrogen to form in divers' bodies and block the flow of blood. (Today, we call this condition, which can affect scuba divers, decompression sickness or "the bends.") Over time, the technology invented to improve the diving bell was adapted for a more sophisticated diving device: the submarine.

Bet You **Didn't Know**

Duck hunters in ancient Egypt used hollow plant reeds as snorkels.

CONCRETE

A Rock-Solid Idea

oday's world is filled with concrete—literally. From sidewalks to roads to bridges to entire buildings, it's everywhere. In fact, it's the most commonly used human-made material in the modern world. But concrete is a surprisingly ancient creation.

YOU DON'T KNOW WHAT YOU'VE GOT TILL **IT'S GONE!**

In A.D. 79, Mount Vesuvius erupted, burying about 2,000 citizens of Pompeii, Italy, alive in volcanic ash. That same substance helped the Romans create the first known concrete, which they made by mixing volcanic ash, burnt limestone, and water into a paste. They poured this mixture into wooden molds, where it set into pieces of concrete.

The ancient Romans' astounding architecture would not have been possible without the incredible strength of the new building material. Concrete was used to build the Colosseum, where emperors watched gladiators fight to the death. It was used for the dome of the famous Pantheon temple, which remains in perfect condition after 1,800 years, and is still the largest unreinforced concrete dome in the world.

When the Roman Empire fell in A.D. 476, the Roman recipe for concrete was lost forever. In fact, engineers still don't know how the Pantheon is standing. For a thousand years, concrete disappeared. To become Earth's number one building material, it had to be re-created from scratch—something that didn't happen until the early 1500s, when an Italian friar studied ancient Roman architecture texts and came up with a new recipe. The building he created—an arched bridge topped with multistory houses—was demolished after 250 years. But the concrete concept held firm. By the 1800s, it was taking over structures worldwide.

Bet You **Didn't Know**

The world's highest concrete dam is the Grande Dixence in Switzerland. It's 935 feet (285 m) tall and is made of 7,800,000 cubic yards (5,960,000 cubic m) of concrete.

Color STORY

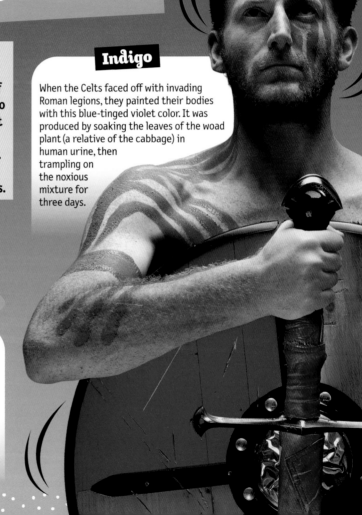

Today, every crayon box contains an astounding array of colors, from deepest blue to boldest red. But for ancient artists, getting the right color wasn't always so easy. Here are some of history's strangest paint ingredients.

Indigo

When the Celts faced off with invading Roman legions, they painted their bodies with this blue-tinged violet color. It was produced by soaking the leaves of the woad plant (a relative of the cabbage) in human urine, then trampling on the noxious mixture for three days.

Pure White

The deadliest white pigment ever produced was made from lead. To create it, ancient artisans had to pack lead strips together with vinegar and animal dung. If they survived the smell, the exposure to toxic lead often killed them.

Bright Yellow

The secret behind this sunny pigment produced in India wasn't widely known until the 19th century: It was made from the urine of cows fed a diet of only mango leaves.

Deep Red

European artists had to do without a vivid red until Europeans invaded South America in the 1500s, where they found the Aztec people sporting fabrics dyed in the deepest red hue. The color came from an insect living inside prickly pear cacti. About 70,000 of the bugs had to be dried, crushed, and dunked in alcohol to produce a pound of the color.

Ultramarine Blue

European painters didn't have an intense blue hue to work with until the rock lapis lazuli was imported there from what is now Afghanistan in the A.D. 900s. Lapis lazuli was more expensive than gold because of its extreme rarity. To this day, the purest grade is still sourced from a single mine.

Brown

At the end of the 19th century, a group of English painters favored a shade of brown made from a bone-chilling source: ground-up mummies. Though it was illegal, untold priceless Egyptian mummies were exported from Egypt to Europe at the time, where they were pulverized and turned into everything from medicine to paint.

HOW **RUDE!**

HOURGLASS

Sands of **Time**

PIRATE FLAG

MWAHAHAHA! RACE AGAINST THIS!

Watch enough movies and you'll see this classic suspenseful scene: The hapless hero strains against his bonds, gaping in horror at the device on the table. Inside, sand trickles in a slow-but-steady stream from one glass bulb down into another. The hourglass shows that time is almost up.

The hourglass seems like it must be very old—thousands of years at least. Even historians thought so, until they discovered that an hourglass depicted in an ancient Roman sculpture was actually a relatively recent addition, added in the 16th century. In fact, the hourglass didn't become widely used until about 700 years ago—about the same time as the mechanical clock!

Back then, people measured time in hours that were not of equal duration, based on the length of the day and night of that particular date. But sailors on a ship needed standard hours, because they used the passage of time to calculate how far they had traveled. Sand-filled hourglasses kept working even when the boat was rocked by waves, so they were perfect for ocean voyages.

The hourglass became not just a practical device, but a potent symbol. Hourglasses appear often in Renaissance art—but they're not timepieces that happen to be in the background; they're emblems of death, reminding people of their limited time on Earth. Later, pirates used the hourglass on their flags as a warning of the fate of anyone who resisted attack. Beware!

RENAISSANCE ART

Bet You **Didn't Know**

Most hourglasses aren't filled with sand, which tends to clump. Instead, they use materials like marble dust or tiny glass beads.

COMPASS

Point the Way

Can you imagine crossing the ocean with only the sun and stars to find your way? Before the compass was invented, that's how ancient explorers had to navigate.

For most of human history, many people who set sail never returned. Bad weather often blotted out the sky, disorienting sailors. In the fourth century A.D., a Roman military writer remarked that the season from June to mid-September was the only time one could sail the Mediterranean Sea with some safety—the rest of the year was too dangerous to even attempt a journey. The compass made it possible to navigate accurately across great distances, allowing humans to sail all seven seas.

Historians think the compass first appeared in China. Two thousand years ago, writings show that Chinese scientists knew that rubbing something made of iron, like a needle, with a naturally occurring magnet, called a lodestone, would cause the needle to become magnetized. By attaching that needle to a piece of wood or cork and floating it in water, the needle would spin until it pointed north and south. When the needle was mounted on a card showing the directions, it became a portable navigation device.

Magnetic compasses revolutionized ocean travel. But early versions weren't foolproof. Earth's magnetic north pole (which is where a compass points) is not the same as its geographic North Pole. To make matters more difficult, magnetic north constantly shifts location as Earth's magnetic field changes—the two poles can be hundreds or even thousands of miles apart. Despite that challenge, explorer Ferdinand Magellan used a compass to lead the first around-the-world expedition in 1519, beginning the age of global exploration.

CIRCUMNAVIGATION IS MY MIDDLE NAME!

FERDINAND MAGELLAN

CATAPULT

Fire Away

WHAT SHALL I FLING NEXT?

Boom! Crash! Uh-oh, m'lord or m'lady, your castle is under siege! What's that dastardly contraption laying waste to your fearsome fortress? It's a catapult, a weapon that changed war forever.

Catapults were invented long before the time of knights and castles— around 400 B.C. The first catapult was likely the product of engineers working for Philip II of Macedonia, father of conqueror Alexander the Great. Their invention was a type of catapult called a ballista: a device like a giant crossbow that shot a spear.

During the Middle Ages, kings began building cities fortified by giant stone walls. Weapons like bows and arrows were no match for these enormous fortresses: Attackers had to have catapults. An arms race started, with royals paying top dollar to inventors who could come up with the latest and greatest in missile-launching technology. Some catapults had wheels for easy maneuverability; others could throw huge stones 300 feet (91 m) or more. People got creative with the ammunition, too, shooting everything from flaming arrows to the diseased dead bodies of cows, which they hoped would infect the castle's inhabitants.

BALLISTA

The sight of a catapult lumbering over the horizon struck fear into hearts everywhere until the 15th century, when gunpowder blew up as the premier weapon of war. But the earlier tool of terror didn't disappear: Modern catapults fling airplanes into the sky from the floating warships we call aircraft carriers.

Lost SECRETS

It might not seem like innovators of today—responsible for incredible technology from supercomputers to 3D printers—could be stumped by inventions from thousands of years ago. But it's true. Here are a few ancient inventions that have baffled generations of the brightest minds.

Greek Fire

Liquid fire that sticks to everything it touches and can't be extinguished with water sounds like the stuff of science fiction. But it was a real weapon fired from Byzantine ships in the seventh century A.D. The recipe was a family secret that was lost when the creators died. Modern-day experts can only guess at the ingredients.

Stone Spheres

In the 1930s, workers started looking for a place to plant banana trees in Costa Rica's Diquís Valley when they stumbled upon something else: hundreds of stone spheres, ranging in size from ones small enough to hold in your hand to ones over six feet (2 m) across. The strangest thing about the stones was that they were perfectly round. Nobody is sure exactly when, why, or how they were made.

Islamic Swords

European knights fighting the medieval Crusades were shocked when they faced off with Islamic fighters wielding strange and powerful swords. According to the tales, they were so sharp they could slice through a floating handkerchief and so flexible they could bend 90 degrees without breaking. Experts still aren't sure what the mystery material was.

Roman Doodad

Was it a candleholder, a flower stand, a game, an instrument—or just decoration? Nobody knows. More than a hundred of these hollow, 12-sided bronze artifacts, called dodecahedra, have been discovered dating back to ancient Rome. One of the only things known about them is that they must have been highly valuable; many were found in treasure hoards.

WHO AM I?

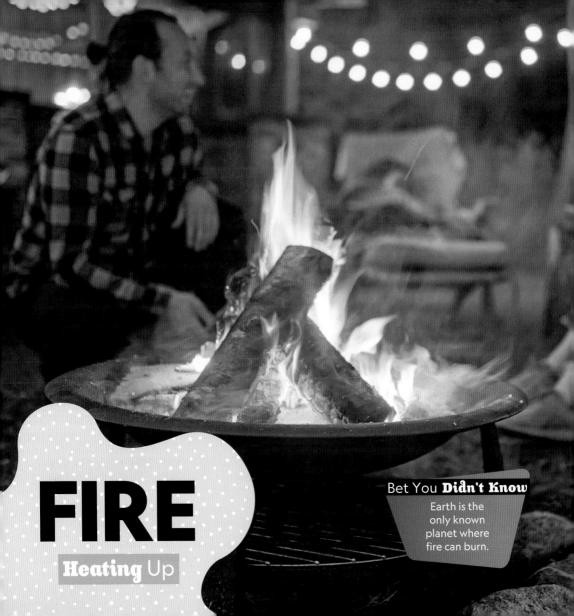

FIRE

Heating Up

WILDFIRE

Twist a knob on your stove or flick a switch on your gas fireplace, and flames will burst forth. Fire changed the course of human history, allowing our ancestors to stay warm, ward off predators, live in harsh climates, and, of course, cook their food.

The first way ancient humans saw the flicker of flames would have been in the form of wildfires. About seven million years ago, Africa—the birthplace of humans—was covered with grassland. Regular wildfires kept it from turning into forest. Our human ancestors living on the savannas would have watched in awe as raging fires consumed the landscape—and then left dead animals and plants in their wake. Ancient people also may have noticed that fire made certain foods tastier and easier to eat.

Experts think it was perhaps about 1.5 million years ago that humans figured out how to contain small flames from wildfires and keep them burning. A cave in South Africa containing plant ash and bone fragments—evidence of cooking—shows that we learned how to control fire at least a million years ago. By about 400,000 years ago, humans had learned to start their own fires by striking chunks of iron against pieces of flint, which experts believe might have happened by accident when they chipped stones into tools.

As time went on, humans got more sophisticated at mastering fire. Ötzi the Iceman, the 5,000-year-old body discovered by hikers in the Italian Alps, carried his fire with him: glowing embers wrapped in maple leaves and carefully stored inside a box made of birchbark. Today, we use fire to make our cars go, heat our homes, and barbecue our burgers.

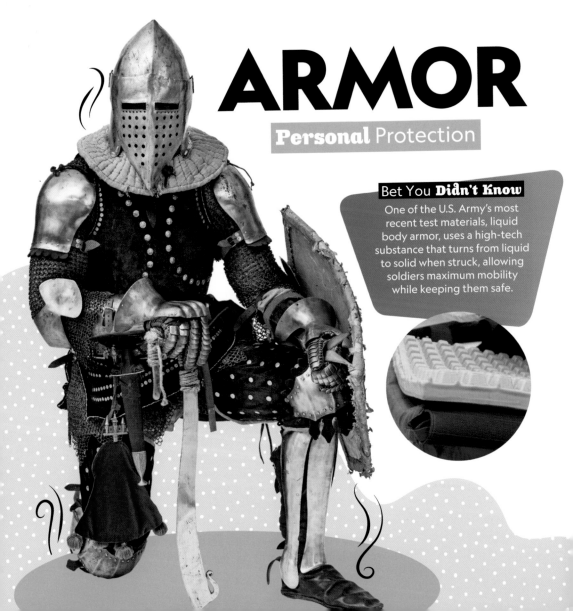

ARMOR

Personal Protection

Bet You **Didn't Know**

One of the U.S. Army's most recent test materials, liquid body armor, uses a high-tech substance that turns from liquid to solid when struck, allowing soldiers maximum mobility while keeping them safe.

From Kevlar vests that stop bullets to glasses that prevent eye damage, armor has come a long way from the time of knights clanking across the battlefield. But you might be surprised to learn that armor is much older than even that.

A STATUE OF A MING DYNASTY WARRIOR

COME AT ME, BRO.

Ancient people discovered that when leather was boiled to stiffen it, it became sturdy enough to fend off blows from zinging arrows and stabbing spears. In the 11th century B.C., Chinese warriors protected themselves with armor made of up to seven layers of rhinoceros skin. Armor technology got a big boost when people realized it was possible to heat and mold metal into new shapes. From around 160 B.C., Roman soldiers wore shirts made of chain mail, small metal rings linked together.

Flexible yet impervious to slashing weapons, chain mail was such an ingenious invention that medieval knights borrowed the technology. As blacksmiths became more skilled, they developed steel plate armor, flat sections of metal joined together. One complete suit of armor from Germany in the early 16th century is a metal suit with flexible joints that covered the wearer from head to toe, with just a slit for the eyes and a few small holes for breathing. This kind of armor made the wearer impervious to nearly any attack, but it was so expensive that only the very wealthy could afford to wear it to war.

History books often teach that medieval armor was hard to move in. Though heavy, it allowed for surprising agility: In 2011, historians found that volunteers wearing replica suits could even perform cartwheels!

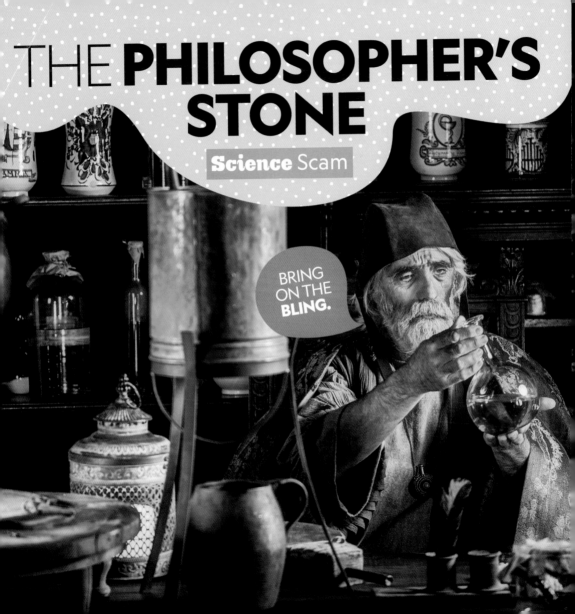

THE PHILOSOPHER'S STONE

STONE

Science Scam

BRING ON THE **BLING.**

This is one object that was never an everyday item. In fact, it never existed at all. But that didn't stop many of history's most brilliant minds from devoting their lives to finding it.

It's fair to say that from the Middle Ages all the way to the late 17th century, people were obsessed with the philosopher's stone: a legendary rock said to have the ability to turn ordinary metals such as iron and tin into precious metals like gold and silver. The whole thing started in 1382, when a French bookseller named Nicolas Flamel claimed to

BLAST! MERCURY AGAIN!

NICOLAS FLAMEL

have decoded an ancient book of alchemy and discovered a recipe for transforming mercury into gold. It seems impossible that the smartest people of the age would have fallen for this tall tale, but that's exactly what happened.

When famed English mathematician Isaac Newton, for example, wasn't discovering the laws of motion or inventing calculus, he was fanatically fixated on finding Flamel's secret. He was so devoted, in fact, that it might have killed him: Newton's final years were plagued by severe insomnia, delusions, and paranoia—possibly side effects of the toxic levels of mercury he exposed himself to in his search for the get-rich-quick rock.

No one ever succeeded at finding the philosopher's stone. But over the course of the wild-goose chase, scientists performed groundbreaking experiments that led to the discovery of elements and formed the foundation of the entire field of chemistry. It may have been a fictional stone, but it resulted in rock-solid science.

Bet You **Didn't Know**

Harry Potter fans might recognize the name of Nicolas Flamel, a character in *Harry Potter and the Philosopher's Stone,* the first book in J. K. Rowling's popular series, which was renamed *Harry Potter and the Sorcerer's Stone* in the United States.

Close to Home

There's nowhere quite so familiar as home. But believe it or not, its history is full of unfamiliar facts. From decor that was unexpectedly deadly, to an appliance that was invented by accident, your house is hiding all kinds of secrets. So curl up on the couch with this chapter—but don't get too comfortable.

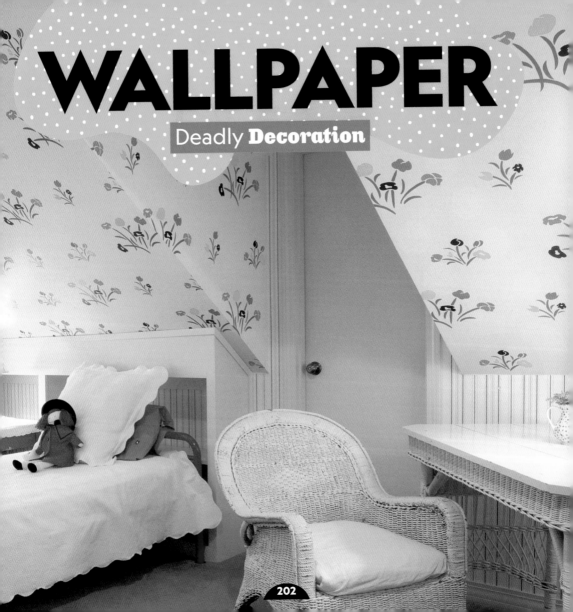

WALLPAPER

Deadly **Decoration**

Striped or floral or depicting quaint scenes from times gone by, wallpaper seems perfectly harmless. But this bit of decorative flair was once nothing short of lethal.

Wallpaper could be found in only the fanciest homes until 1830, when a tax that had made it extremely expensive was lifted. Suddenly, millions of people started decorating their rooms with charming prints. At the same time, droves started dying from a mysterious illness.

In 1862, for example, a London couple lost all four of their children over the course of just a few months. Doctors were baffled—though one did observe that the children's bedroom was papered in wallpaper in a vivid yellowish green color. The shade, called Scheele's green, was extremely popular at the time. It was used to dye all sorts of objects, from candles to baby carriages. It was also laced with arsenic, a chemical so toxic that merely sleeping in the same room with it could kill.

By the late 19th century, an astounding 80 percent of English wallpapers contained deadly arsenic. Victorian women painted their faces with arsenic-filled cosmetics, and the stuff was sprayed on meat and vegetables to deter insects. It was even an ingredient in "lickable" postage stamps. Despite the danger, people liked the hue so much that they waited to tear out their toxic wallpaper until the end of the 19th century.

Bet You **Didn't Know**

Some historians think French military leader Napoleon Bonaparte was poisoned to death by his wallpaper.

AIR-CONDITIONING

Chilling Out

SOME RELIEF **AT LAST!**

Bet You **Didn't Know**

In the early days of air-conditioning, moviemakers began releasing their biggest hits during summer, when they were sure to be seen by the big audiences that flocked to air-conditioned movie theaters. The "summer blockbuster" is still around today.

*A*aaah. There's nothing like the feeling of walking inside an air-conditioned building on a hot day. Ancient people thought so, too: The inhabitants of northwest India, for example, built huge cooling pools of water in the bases of their structures 1,500 years ago. But somewhere along the way attitudes shifted. In some parts of the world, people became downright skeptical of the idea of cooling the air, thinking it was unnatural. As late as the early 1900s, members of the U.S. Congress decided not to install air-conditioning in the Capitol because they were worried voters would laugh at them for not being able to take the heat!

Even so, people longed to cool off. For hundreds of years, inventors tinkered with ideas for air-conditioning. In the 17th century, one named Cornelius Drebbel put on a demonstration in which he mixed snow with water, salt, and potassium nitrate to form ice crystals and cool down London's Westminster Abbey. Reports say that King James, who was in the audience, ran out of the building, shivering.

Two centuries later, U.S. president James A. Garfield was shot on July 2, 1881. As the president slowly died over the course of that summer, engineers looked for a way to keep him cool to relieve his suffering. An astronomer named Simon Newcomb built a fan that blew air over a giant bucket of ice. It went through hundreds of pounds of ice an hour, but could cool a room down by 20 degrees Fahrenheit (11 degrees Celsius).

I AM BRRR-ILLIANT!

SIMON NEWCOMB

The idea caught on. Modern air-conditioning—which works by circulating a chemical called a refrigerant inside and outside of a house, absorbing and casting off heat as it goes—debuted to the public in 1939. Then, at the New York World's Fair, 65,000 people cooled down in an air-conditioned "Igloo of Tomorrow." The thrill of chill proved too much to resist: By the 1960s, millions of air conditioners were sold every year.

LIGHTNING
ROD

It's **Electric**

They say that lightning never strikes the same place twice—but it's not true. The Empire State Building, for example, jolts from bolts about 23 times a year. So how is the monument still standing?

Founding Father Benjamin Franklin was obsessed with thunder and lightning. During the 1700s, he could often be spotted chasing storms on horseback. He turned his home into a laboratory of electricity, accidentally shocking himself out cold more than once. Noticing that a pointed metal needle could pull electricity from a charged object, Franklin became convinced that a metal rod would draw electricity down from the clouds, where it would strike the rod instead of buildings, trees, or people.

Not everyone was convinced. English scientists decreed that lightning rods should be blunt-tipped, not pointed as in Franklin's model. King George III even had this version installed on his palace. When it came time for the colonists to install their own lightning rods, they went with Franklin's pointed rods in a show of rebellion against the hated king.

Franklin's lightning rods went on to protect buildings and homes all around the United States. They became so trendy that fashionable women even started wearing them, sporting decorative lightning rods attached to their hats. Now that's shocking style!

WATT AN INVENTION!

BENJAMIN FRANKLIN

Bet You **Didn't Know**

Franklin's other inventions included a mechanical arm to reach books on high shelves, the rocking chair, a smokeless fireplace, and a pulley system that allowed him to lock and unlock his bedroom door without getting out of bed.

EVERY TIME IT STRIKES, I PROTECT **MY CITY!**

THEY CAME FROM Space

What does your house have in common with a spaceship? More than you might think. Many ordinary household items are the result of technology developed for space missions. These items might be familiar, but their origins are truly far-out!

NOW I CAN ENJOY MY HIKE AND DRINK **FRESH NATURAL WATER ON EARTH!**

Water Filtration

In space, every drop of water has to be reused—so, yep, that means astronauts drink their recycled urine! The filtration technology has made its way into all kinds of Earth-based devices, including water bottles that purify water from lakes and streams so it's safe for campers to drink.

Memory Foam

Aaah. There's nothing quite like sinking into a memory foam mattress. But the material wasn't invented for sleep—instead, it originally cushioned seats for test pilots, protecting their bodies from the extreme g-forces of takeoff. Today, memory foam can be found not just in mattresses, but also shoes, movie theater seats, and football helmets.

Smoke Detector

NASA needed a way to alert astronauts to possible toxic gas leaks in its first space station, Skylab. But the device couldn't be too sensitive, or it would go off every time the crew heated up some freeze-dried food. Today, a modern version of the invention keeps you safe from fire—without beeping every time you use the stove.

Home Insulation

In space, outside temperatures range from 400°F (204°C) to minus 400°F (-240°C). To protect astronauts from roasting or freezing, spacecraft need superior insulation. Today, the same barrier that was built into the Apollo spacecraft keeps the temperature of many houses comfortable.

Dustbuster

When astronauts first began to explore the moon, they needed an instrument for taking samples—and since there are no electrical outlets on the lunar surface, the device had to be battery-powered. Their handheld, cordless machine was adapted to create all kinds of Earth-based devices, including the small battery-powered vacuum known as the Dustbuster.

REMOTE CONTROL

Game **Changer**

OK, who stole the remote? If you were watching TV before 1955, the answer would be no one—because remotes hadn't been invented yet!

Today, it seems hard to believe that when people wanted to change the channel, they had to get up and walk across the room to the TV. But the reason the remote was invented wasn't to allow viewers to stay on the sofa—it was to avoid the commercials. Apparently, ads in the 1950s were just as annoying as they are today, because a U.S. electronics company president got so fed up that he challenged his engineers to devise a device that would allow him to mute them or skip to another channel.

In response, the engineers came up with the world's first remote control, called the Flash-Matic. During this time, futuristic contraptions were the height of cool. So the Flash-Matic was designed to look like a space-age ray gun, and it used a zap of light to trigger sensors on the TV. The only problem was that other light sources could trigger the sensors, too, so many people found the sun changing the channels against their will.

A new model, called the Space Command, featured four buttons mounted on a sleek plastic rectangle. It communicated with the TV using ultrasonics—sounds too high for the human ear to hear. But the simplicity of that design didn't stick around—today's remotes often contain nearly 100 buttons! (What does "FREEZE" do, anyway?)

GUESS WHO IS IN **CHARGE!**

Bet You **Didn't Know**

Some state-of-the-art toilets now come with a remote control to heat the seat, blow hot air, and play music.

LAUNDRY
CHUTE

A Hidden **History**

HOW DID WE **GET HERE?**

Some old houses sport a laundry chute, a tunnel from the upper floors down to the basement. Throughout its history, this hidden passageway has been used not just to transport dirty linens, but to hide secrets.

No one is sure when or where the first laundry chute was invented. Some experts say that before laundry chutes were built into houses, people used to insert fabric sleeves through the gaps between walls and use them to drop laundry down to lower floors. Around the early 20th century, laundry chutes had become top-of-the-line features that apartments buildings advertised to entice new tenants.

But just as some people decided laundry chutes were a handy way to deal with the wash, others realized they also made a good place to stash stuff they didn't want found. In 1945, a homeowner in Kansas City, Missouri, U.S.A., opened her basement chute to find not just her soiled linen but also $1,920 that had recently been stolen from one of her houseguests. The police believed the thief, fearing capture, had dropped the money and fled the scene of the crime.

In 2006, two Russian assassins traveled to a U.K. hotel to take out an opponent using radioactive polonium. Apparently not realizing they were handling the most toxic substance known to man, they tossed a poison-soaked towel down the hotel's laundry chute. The toxic towel contained enough radioactive material in every square inch (6.5 sq cm) to kill six adult men. Now that's some dirty laundry!

STEP AWAY FROM THE **TOWELS!**

FURNITURE

Take a **Seat**

When you pull up to the table for dinner or flop on your bed at night, you probably don't give a second thought to the furniture beneath you. But you really should, because for most of human history, beds and tables as we know them didn't exist.

The first piece of furniture may have been the bed. Ancient Egyptians slept on woven cords secured to simple wooden bed frames. Around the 16th century B.C., Egyptian beds sloped upward, and people slept with their heads elevated. A wooden footboard at the bottom kept them from sliding off in their sleep.

The beds discovered in the tomb of the pharaoh Tutankhamun were built so they could be easily taken apart and reassembled. That's because when pharaohs traveled around their lands, they took their furniture with them. That on-the-move mentality remained popular until medieval

WELCOME TO MY **ABODE!**

times began in Europe in the fifth century A.D. Since nobles were almost constantly traveling between their many estates, their furniture was designed to be mobile. The Italian word for furniture is even *mobilia*.

People stored their belongings in trunks, which had domed lids to keep water from getting in during travel. (It wasn't until the 1600s that someone thought to fit drawers into a trunk and make the first dresser.) Once they arrived at their destination, all of medieval living took place in one large room called the hall. At mealtimes, people sat on benches and balanced simple boards across their knees to create a table as they ate. At night, they would heap some straw into a pile, find a blanket, and settle in for the night—that's why we "make the bed" today.

Bet You **Didn't Know**

In the 1700s, it was considered stylish to arrange your tables and chairs up against the room's walls—like a modern waiting room.

Pet PAST

They're our daily companions, sharing our homes, stealing the best spot on the couch, and always hoping for a belly rub. For many people, it's hard to imagine home life without pets. But what's the story of how cats and dogs went from wild animals to loving companions?

I LOVE MY **HUMAN!**

Cats

In 2004, archaeologists found a 9,500-year-old grave on the Mediterranean island of Cyprus. Inside were the remains of a human and a pet cat, lovingly buried together along with seashells and polished stones. But experts think the partnership between cats and people is even older than that, stretching back to about 12,000 years ago. That's when humans were first beginning to farm in the region known today as the Middle East. While farming allowed people to save precious food to last through the winter, stored food was an easy target for mice and other small animals. These pests became a real problem for ancient humans. Luckily, cats came to the rescue.

Wild cats from the nearby forests crept into human villages, enticed by the buffet of prey. They ate the rodents that ate the food, and so humans encouraged their furry pest control to stay around, occasionally tossing the wild cats some tasty leftovers. Over thousands of years, it became the *purr*-fect partnership.

Dogs

Experts aren't sure when the first wolf came out of the woods and became a domestic dog, but they do know it was very long ago. Recent genetic analysis shows that dogs split off from gray wolves as long as about 40,000 years ago. Other scientists think they were first tamed about 15,000 years ago. Either way, dogs were the first domesticated animals, becoming our partners before we herded goats, cows, pigs, or sheep.

Dogs are also the only large carnivore ever to be domesticated (modern house cats are considered semidomesticated). Their sharp teeth and strong jaws would have been a safety hazard for ancient people. So why did we become friends? Experts think that, like cats, dogs started hanging around humans because of the promise of an easier life. Maybe they stole bones from our trash heaps or ventured close enough to the fire to snag an offered snack. Over time, humans realized how useful dogs could be, and they were trained for herding, tracking, hunting, and even war. Along the way, they became our friends.

CARPET

Fancy **Floors**

WOOL YOU LOOK AT THAT?!

Today, we think of home as a place to get cozy. But before the 18th century, the idea of being comfortable was so unfamiliar that there wasn't even an English word for it.

So it's no wonder that for most of European history, people didn't have anything soft and snug underfoot. Until nearly the 20th century, most houses had bare earth or stone floors. To provide a bit of warmth and cushioning, they were covered with straw. The straw collected food remnants, body waste from people and animals, and insects and rodents. But people rarely removed the old, dirty straw, instead simply adding a new layer from time to time.

In other parts of the world, people had been making carpets long before this. One 2,500-year-old example, the oldest carpet ever found, was pulled from a royal tomb in southern Siberia. Historians think that nomadic shepherds in Persia (modern-day Iran) and Central Asia may have hand-knotted wool from their animals into carpets even earlier. These carpets were sometimes laid on the ground, but were also used as coverings for walls and doorways, and as blankets.

When the fine rugs from this part of the world were first brought to Europe in the 12th century, they were far too precious to be stepped on. Rugs were sometimes hung on walls or unfurled on tables—but often, they were kept safely stored away and only brought out to show off to special guests.

MAKING **HAY!**

Bet You **Didn't Know**

In medieval times, a deep layer of straw signaled that the home belonged to a person wealthy enough to splurge on it. The French would say that a rich man was "waist-deep in straw."

CHAPTER 9 • Close to Home

I n ancient times, if you wanted to hide away something important you'd squirrel it up a tree, put it in a cave, or bury it underground.

Starting in the eighth century A.D., European nobles would put their jewels and other valuables in wooden chests. Of course, a thief who knew where to look could simply open the box and make away with the goods. So storage chests couldn't be truly secure until they had locking lids. That happened around the 16th century, when German craftsmen began producing locking iron strongboxes reinforced with interlaced metal bands. Because some people wrongly believed that these boxes had once housed the treasures of the Spanish Armada (a fleet of ships that sailed in the 1500s), they were called Armada chests.

In the 17th and 18th centuries, people started thinking up even smarter ways to deter thieves. The

A GERMAN CHEST SHOWING A COMPLEX LOCKING SYSTEM

coffers used by nobles at that time had complex locking mechanisms that would often take up the entire inside of the lid. The keyhole at the front was usually a decoy—the real one would be concealed beneath a panel.

From the 1860s to the 1890s, bands of roving outlaws in the American Wild West would enter banks and force tellers to hand over the keys to the strongbox or reveal the lock's combination. To keep criminals from forcing tellers to open the safe, safes were outfitted with time locks, which didn't use keys and could only open at specific times of day. Today, banks protect their valuables with heat detectors, magnetic fields, and locks with millions of possible combinations.

MICROWAVES

*B**eep beep beep!** **Your food is ready.** Today, microwaves are such a standard part of the kitchen that about 96 percent of U.S. homes include one. So it's somewhat surprising that this appliance was invented by accident.*

Microwaves were cooked up from radar technology. First used during World War II, radar was based on the idea that radio waves will bounce off the surfaces of large objects. By shooting out radio waves in a certain direction and waiting to see if any bounced back, radar could detect the presence of planes and ships even when they were obscured by fog, clouds, or the dark of night. It was a major breakthrough in military technology.

After the war, America had many leftover magnetrons—the device that produces the radio waves—and no use for them. Luckily, an engineer named Percy Spencer stumbled upon a new idea. One day in 1946, he was experimenting with one when he

MMM, **POPCORN!**

RADAR RANGE

noticed that a candy bar in his pocket had melted. Could the magnetron be the cause? Spencer pointed the magnetron at corn kernels, which popped, and then at an egg, which heated up so fast it exploded.

Realizing he had something hot on his hands, Spencer designed the first microwave oven, which he called the Radar Range. The size of a refrigerator and costing $5,000, it wasn't right for home cooks. But countertop models were released in 1967, and now, it's hard to find a kitchen without one!

CHAPTER **10**

Devices & Doodads

Have you ever wondered why a computer keyboard is laid out in such a confusing order? Or what the first thing to come out of a vending machine was? Then read on. There are secret stories hiding in everything around you—and these are some of the strangest of all.

BILLBOARDS

Scaled to Sell

HAVE YOU **LOST** A TREASURED **CHEW TOY?**

CALL **DOGGY DETECTIVES!**
We'll sniff it out or you get your money back!

Bet You **Didn't Know**

Billboards on the Sunset Strip in Los Angeles can cost companies more than $100,000 per month to run.

TALK ABOUT A HUGE **PROMOTION!**

oday, most advertisements are digital. They can often be scrolled past, deleted, or at least muted. But there's one form of real-life ad that still stands tall: billboards.

People were posting advertisements on roadsides by the early 1800s. They alerted travelers on foot or horseback to nearby inns where they could get a clean bed and a warm meal. The idea of posted advertising spread, and in 1835, people gawked at the first large-scale ad, measuring more than 50 square feet (4.7 sq m), and illustrating the splendors of a circus.

But billboards really went big when the car replaced the horse during the early 20th century. Since people were traveling at higher speeds and looking at the landscape from farther away, roadside advertising had to be huge if it wanted to

BILLBOARDS IN 1890

get noticed. By 1899, a sign hawking Lea & Perrins Worcestershire sauce stretched for almost half a mile (0.6 km) along the Erie Basin in New York City. Just a decade later, the United States had so many billboards that if they had been laid end to end, they would stretch from Florida to Maine.

Today, billboards get creative with visual effects like moving messages and 3D characters. One billboard in Brazil even uses fluorescent lights and chemical scent to attract—and then zap—disease-carrying mosquitoes. Now that's an ad that gets results!

THAT **SUCKS!**

FERTILIZER

Food for Thought

It's something you've probably never paid much attention to. But without fertilizer, experts estimate that two out of every five people on Earth—the populations of China, India, and the United States combined—would not be alive today. That's potent stuff.

People have fertilized their crops with animal waste for at least 8,000 years. It might seem gross to feed plants poo, but manure contains all sorts of nutrients—most importantly, nitrogen—that help crops grow strong and healthy. Manure made the perfect fertilizer—that is, until the beginning of the 20th century, when we started to run out.

WASTE NOT, WANT NOT!

FRITZ HABER

That was when experts calculated how fast the population was growing and discovered something alarming: We would soon have far more mouths to feed than food to feed them. Humans needed a way to grow more food fast, and without using more farmland. It seemed like an impossible problem. But in 1908, German scientist Fritz Haber solved it, devising a way to pull nitrogen from the air to create human-made fertilizer. Today, it's considered one of the most important inventions ever.

Nitrogen fertilizer helped feed the modern world—but it has a dark side, too. We now use so much that it leaches out of farmlands and contaminates our water and air. Scientists are experimenting with smarter ways to use nitrogen fertilizer so it can help support planet Earth's growing population without harm.

Bet You **Didn't Know**

Nearly all of the air we breathe—about 80 percent—is not made of oxygen, but nitrogen.

229

COMPUTER KEYBOARDS

Fast **Fingers**

THE QUICK BROWN FOX ...

The first time you looked at a computer keyboard, you probably wondered: Why isn't it in alphabetical order? As we text and type, we get used to the layout of the letters. The design of the modern keyboard might seem baffling—unless you know the story behind it!

The first typewriter, invented in 1867, had the alphabet and punctuation marks laid out in two rows. It seemed like the most logical order—since people already knew the alphabet, they wouldn't waste time hunting for the right key. There are several versions of what happened next, but the most popular one says that there was one problem: The keys were mounted on metal arms, and if the user hit one

FIRST TYPEWRITER

The new design meant it took longer for typists to hit the right keys, which minimized jams. It also meant the keyboard was purposefully laid out to be as hard to use as possible. But by 1890, QWERTY was in use on more than 100,000 typewriters across the United States.

There have been many rival designs introduced, including the Dvorak Simplified Keyboard in the 1930s, which claimed to enable faster, more accurate typing with minimal finger motion. But by then it was too late—QWERTY ruled the world.

key after another too quickly, the arms would run into each other, causing the delicate machine to jam up. To solve the problem, inventor Christopher Latham Sholes redesigned the keyboard, separating the most common sequences of letters, like "th" and "he." The new keyboard was named QWERTY for the six letters in the top left corner.

Bet You **Didn't Know**

The word "typewriter" can be typed using only the top row of letters on a QWERTY keyboard.

QWERTY KEYBOARD

Camping OUT

T he next time you pack your tent and provisions for a camping trip, consider all the supplies you have available to make your voyage into the great outdoors easier. Before modern times, campers didn't have waterproof sleeping bags or even reliable flashlights. Here's how these cool camping creations came to be.

Flashlight

The original flashlight, invented in 1899, had three D batteries end to end inside a tube-shaped handle, with a lightbulb at one end. But early batteries were so weak that the light could only stay on for a brief period, which is how the device earned the name "flashlight."

Duffel Bag

People have long searched for ways to collect and carry their belongings. Early bags were made of animal skins or wool, but they let in rain and snow. In the early 17th century, Spanish and Portuguese sailors figured out that bags made from leftover scraps of their sails kept out rain and seawater. The coarse wool cloth was sturdy and waterproof, and it was imported from the town of Duffel, Belgium.

WATER IS LIFE!

Water Pack

You'd never go hiking without water, right? Well, even Paleolithic people were clued in to that. They crafted early versions of the water bottle out of animal bladders, the part of the body that holds urine. That might seem gross, but they were light, flexible, and watertight: the perfect vessel.

Sleeping Bag

In the 1800s, sleeping bags were made of blankets that were lined with sheepskin and had waterproof rubber bottoms to keep out moisture. They were also literal bags, with a hole at the top and no way to open the sides, making them really hard to wiggle in and out of. In 1876, a Welsh inventor named Pryce Pryce-Jones made a wool version that fastened on the side. He produced 60,000 of them for the Russian Army, but they canceled part of their order, leaving him holding 17,000 empty bags. Luckily for Pryce-Jones, the sleeping bags became very popular among British soldiers and Australians in the outback. From there, they spread to campers around the globe.

Air Mattress

If you're lucky enough to snooze on an air mattress while camping, you can thank steamship travelers of the late 1800s. They swapped out traditional mattresses for air-filled ones that could be deflated and stored easily on the cramped quarters of a ship. Bonus: They could serve as emergency life rafts.

VENDING MACHINES

Snacks on Demand

It's a modern scene of almost comical frustration: A person puts in their money and enters the code, the coils start turning—sweet satisfaction is almost at hand—and ... silence. *Nooo!* The treat or drink is *stuck.* It's a vending machine! But how did this convenient dispensing device (and sometimes source of irritation) come to be?

Vending machines might seem like a modern invention, but in fact they originated all the way back in the first century A.D. Greek inventor Heron of Alexandria wanted to come up with a way to stop people from taking more than their fair share of holy water when visiting temples. A coin inserted into his device would trigger a lever to open a valve and dispense a small amount of sacred liquid.

It took the rest of the world about 1,800 years to catch on to the idea. The first coin-operated vending machines, placed in railway stations and post offices around London in 1883, allowed people to purchase envelopes, postcards, and paper on the go. Vending machines hit the United States a few years later, selling gum on subway platforms in New York City.

Starting in Philadelphia, Pennsylvania, U.S.A., in 1902, completely coin-operated diners called automats sold sandwiches, pie, and coffee cake. They became America's first major fast-food chain restaurants. Today, vending machines sell everything from cupcakes to live fishing bait.

Bet You Didn't Know

There are more than five million vending machines in Japan, selling all kinds of items, including fresh eggs, live rhinoceros beetles, and toilet paper.

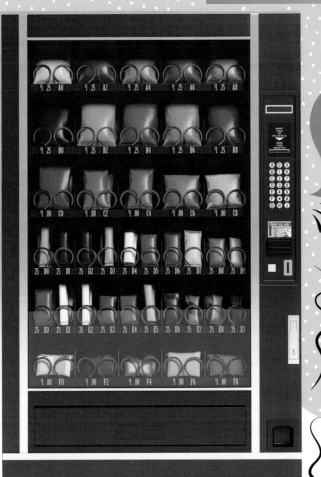

I'VE GOT
SNACKS
ON
SNACKS!

BUBBLE WRAP

A **Poppin'** History

TALK ABOUT DECOR THAT **POPS!**

Of course bubble wrap is irresistibly fun to pop with your fingers. But it's also used to cushion and protect all kinds of items to keep them from breaking during transport. So it might come as a surprise that bubble wrap was intended to be something totally different: wallpaper!

In 1957, decorating with wallpaper was considered the height of cool. So two inventors named Al Fielding and Marc Chavannes decided they'd come up with the next big wallpaper trend: one with 3D texture. They glued two shower curtains together, sealing them so that air bubbles remained in between. But the wallpaper didn't sell.

Their decorating dreams dashed, Fielding and Chavannes decided their product could instead make the perfect insulating material for greenhouses, where the built-in air bubbles would hold in heat and keep plants growing in the off-season. That didn't work either. But three years after the initial invention, a marketer at Sealed Air, the company that made the product, hit on the perfect use. He thought Bubble Wrap would make the best material to protect brand-new IBM computers that were about to be shipped out.

Today, about $400 million worth of Bubble Wrap is sold every year. But the original product may not be around for much longer: In 2015, the Sealed Air company rolled out a new product called iBubble Wrap. It's not inflated until it's ready to be used, which saves tons of space when shipping. Ready for the bad news? It's unpoppable.

LOOK OUT **BELOW!**

Bet You **Didn't Know**

In 2000, people at an Iowa, U.S.A., pumpkin-dropping contest dropped an 815-pound (370-kg) pumpkin from the top of a crane onto a landing pad made of Bubble Wrap. The pumpkin, nicknamed "Gourdzilla," survived the fall.

PAPER
CUPS

Sip **Secrets**

CAN I INTEREST YOU IN A SPOT OF GERMS?

TIN DIPPER

Nowadays, many modern people carry around a personal supply of drinking water in a reusable bottle. And while you might let a friend or family member take the occasional drink from your bottle, you'd probably hesitate to share it with a whole host of strangers. But that's exactly what everyone did before the invention of the paper cup.

Before the 1900s, there were no water fountains. If you wanted to get a drink in a school, train station, or other public place, you would sip water out of a cup called a tin dipper. Since the dipper had touched the lips of untold others before you came along, it was certainly crawling with germs. By the end of the century, scientists discovered that communal cups were spreading deadly diseases like cholera and diphtheria.

One particularly grossed-out individual was an inventor from Boston, Massachusetts, U.S.A., named Lawrence Luellen. He came up with a design for a simple paper cup treated with a waxy substance called paraffin to make it waterproof. People really grabbed on to the idea after the influenza pandemic of 1918 wiped out about 5 percent of the world's population.

It was a simple invention, but it revolutionized the way we look at products, bringing on the disposable age. The invention of paper cups ushered in a whole host of throwaway products, from razors to chopsticks. Today, those products fill the world's dumps—but when they first began, they helped save lives by stopping the spread of disease.

Bet You Didn't Know

Less than one percent of Earth's water is drinkable.

SO DON'T LEAVE THE FAUCET RUNNING!

AHEAD OF THEIR Time

These inventions were so ingenious they had the potential to change the world. The only problem? They were dreamed up too early. These creations were largely dismissed in their time but were hailed as incredible technologies years later.

Parachute

Leonardo da Vinci was perhaps history's most radical inventor. More than 500 years ago, he drew designs for all kinds of ahead-of-their-times inventions—including a parachute made of linen stretched over a pyramid-shaped structure of wooden poles. In the year 2000, a daredevil named Adrian Nichols built a prototype based on the drawings and threw himself out of a hot-air balloon to test it. It worked perfectly.

Earthquake Detector

Today, thousands of instruments called seismometers monitor Earth for the motion of earthquakes, called seismic waves. The original seismometer was invented about 2,000 years ago by a Chinese astronomer, mathematician, and engineer named Zhang Heng. The instrument was a bronze vessel almost six feet (1.8 m) across. Along its outside were eight dragons representing the points on a compass. Each had a small bronze ball in its mouth, positioned above eight open-mouthed toads. When the instrument sensed an earthquake, one of the balls would drop, alerting observers to the location of the earthquake's origin.

Flushing Toilet

In the late 16th century, England's Queen Elizabeth had the very latest in bathroom technology installed in her palace: a flushing toilet. But she was behind the times—the invention was pioneered much earlier, around 2000 B.C.! At that time, the ancient Minoans on the island of Crete were already using flowing water to wash away their waste.

SPEEDCHARGE

Computer and Computer Programming

YOU'RE WELCOME, **KIDS!**

In the 1820s—nearly 200 years before computers became commonplace—a British mathematician named Charles Babbage designed one. His device, called the Analytical Engine, could be programmed to calculate mathematical problems mechanically. And its first program was invented by a mathematician named Ada Lovelace. She realized Babbage's machine was capable of more than even the inventor himself grasped, and predicted that someday computers would compose music, make graphics, and be used for science—all of which came true.

ADA LOVELACE

Electric Car

LARGE AND IN **CHARGE!**

Today, electric cars are just starting to become mainstream vehicles. But they first hit the road more than 100 years ago, when an American chemist named William Morrison created an electric-powered vehicle that could carry six passengers at a blistering top speed of 14 miles an hour (23 km/h). By 1900, one-third of all cars on the road were electric, only to be overtaken by gas-powered versions.

ELECTRIC CAR

SUNGLASSES

Throwing Shade

Sure, sunglasses shield your eyes, but there's no denying that sometimes we slide on a pair of shades because they look cool, too. How did protective eyewear get its super-stylish reputation?

During the Ming dynasty, from 1368 to 1644, the Chinese wore sunglasses with lenses made of darkened quartz. But they weren't for blocking out the sun. According to tradition, Chinese judges weren't supposed to let anybody know what they were thinking as they evaluated evidence. So they donned the eyewear to hide their expressions in the courtroom.

In the 18th century—and possibly much earlier—the Inuit people of the Arctic wore snow goggles to protect their eyes from the glare of the sun off the snowy landscape. These didn't have lenses—instead, they were made of pieces of whalebone or walrus ivory with narrow horizontal slits cut across the center to block out most of the light. Hey, they may not have been fashionable, but they were practical!

In the 1920s, movie stars wore sunglasses to shield their eyes from the blinding flash of early paparazzi cameras. Then, in the 1940s, Air Force pilots started wearing a style of sunglasses called aviators to protect their eyes from the glare during high-altitude battles. People started sliding on shades to copy their favorite celebrities and heroes, and sunglasses are still considered the ultimate cool accessory.

INUIT SNOW GOGGLES

I LOOK
SPEC-TACULAR!

Bet You **Didn't Know**

In the 18th century, green-tinted sunglasses were marketed to the elderly as a way to improve vision. Cool shades, Grandpa!

243

NONSTICK
COOKWARE

A **Slick** Story

It coats cookware, allowing you to slide a fried egg right off the pan and onto your plate with no sticking. Teflon, the trade name for the nonstick surface, is the slipperiest solid material on Earth. And its invention was an accident.

In 1938, chemist Roy Plunkett was working to discover a new kind of refrigerant, a substance that cools by absorbing heat. When he got to the end of the workday, he left a canister of gas he'd been experimenting with sitting out overnight. When he came back the next morning, he noticed something strange: The gas was gone. Plunkett sawed open the canister and found

that the gas had solidified into a waxy white dust later known as polytetrafluoroethylene, or PTFE. Curious, he tried blasting it with corrosive chemicals and extreme temperatures. It was unharmed—and it was also incredibly slippery.

But it took until 1954 for anybody to realize that PTFE would make the perfect cookware coating. Then, a French housewife named Colette Grégoire watched as her husband used the Teflon he'd heard about from an engineer friend to protect his fishing gear from wear and tear. Grégoire asked her husband if he could do the same thing to her pots and pans. Deciding they

THIS IS PAN-TASTIC!

had a new product on their hands, the pair formed a company and started selling it.

When people realized nonstick pots and pans allowed them to make meals with minimal scrubbing afterward, they became a huge hit. A New York City department store sold out of its first 200 pans in two days. These days, PTFE isn't just for cookware—it's been used to coat everything from spaceships to artificial blood vessels.

Bet You **Didn't Know**

The most challenging thing about working with nonstick coating is getting it to stick to the pan.

TELEPHONE

Call on Me

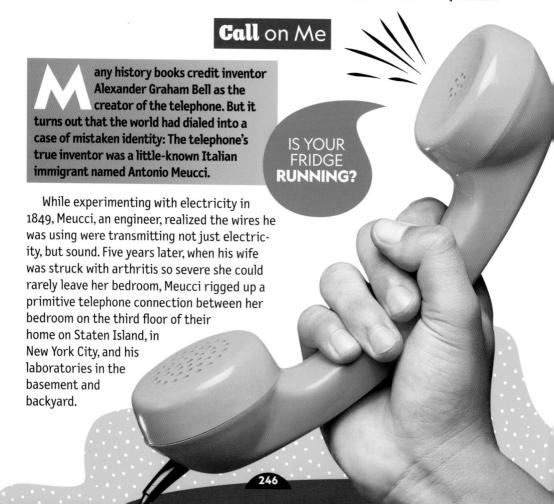

Many history books credit inventor Alexander Graham Bell as the creator of the telephone. But it turns out that the world had dialed into a case of mistaken identity: The telephone's true inventor was a little-known Italian immigrant named Antonio Meucci.

IS YOUR FRIDGE **RUNNING?**

While experimenting with electricity in 1849, Meucci, an engineer, realized the wires he was using were transmitting not just electricity, but sound. Five years later, when his wife was struck with arthritis so severe she could rarely leave her bedroom, Meucci rigged up a primitive telephone connection between her bedroom on the third floor of their home on Staten Island, in New York City, and his laboratories in the basement and backyard.

In the years that followed, Meucci fell on hard times. He lost most of his money, and then tragedy struck in 1871 when he was injured in a ferry accident. To pay for medication, Meucci's wife sold the contents of his lab, including the telephone. Meucci didn't give up. He made a new prototype and, unable to pay the $250 to file a patent, applied for a temporary one. But Meucci couldn't afford to renew his patent, and he lost it in 1874.

In 1876, Alexander Graham Bell filed a patent for the telephone. Meucci—whose materials were stored in the same laboratory where Bell conducted his experiments—accused Bell of stealing his idea.

JUSTICE AT LAST

ANTONIO MEUCCI

He sued, but died before the case could be closed. In 2002, the U.S. Congress passed a resolution declaring Meucci the true inventor of the telephone.

Bet You **Didn't Know**

He may not have really come up with the telephone, but Alexander Graham Bell did invent an early version of fiber optics, a primitive airplane, and a metal detector, which he made in an attempt to locate the bullet that eventually killed U.S. president James Garfield.

ALEXANDER GRAHAM BELL

YOU BETTER **CATCH** IT!

INDEX

Boldface indicates illustrations.

PHOTO CREDITS

Vineeth Roshan/SS; 88 (LE), SSPL/GI; 88 (CTR), BI; 88-89 (UP), Science & Society Picture Library/GI; 89 (RT), Science & Society Picture Library/GI; 89 (LO), Surgical tool box/AL; 90, Chronicle/AL; 91 (LE), 1001nights/GI; 91 (RT), Universal History Archive/GI; 92, Jim Incledon/Fitzpatrick Referrals; 93 (UP), Gado Images AL; 93 (RT), Waxwaxwax/GI; 94, FatCamera/GI; 95 (LE), Cosmin Manci/SS; 95 (RT), New York Public Library/Science Source; 96 (LE), 2707195204/AS; 96 (RT), Scientifica/GI; 97 (UP), Dani Vincek/SS; 97 (RT), Jacobs Stock Photography Ltd/GI; 97 (LO), JosepPerianes/SS; 98, The Picture Art Collection/AL; 99, ktaylorg/GI; 100 (UP), Madlen/SS; 100 (LO), BI; 101 (boat), Africa Studio/AS; 101 (LE), Christian Jung/AS; 101 (CTR), Shawn Hempel/AS; 101 (RT), Grigorita Ko/SS; 101 (LO), mokokomo/SS; 102 (UP), Guniita/Dreamstime; 102 (LO), Dorling Kindersley/UIG/BI; 103, Philippe Turpin/GI; **Chapter 5:** 104 (UP), lotus_studio/AS; 104 (LE), Greg Lawler/GI; 104 (LO), kawephoto/SS; 104-105 (CTR), Richard Griffin/AS; 105 (UP), voloshin311/AS; 105 (LO), Svetlana Foote/Dreamstime; 106 (UP LE), vadarshop/AS; 106 (UP RT), ptnphotof/AS; 106 (LO), De Agostini Picture Library/GI; 107, Ackab Photography/SS; 107 (inset), Hong Vo/SS; 108, Floortje/GI; 109 (UP), francesco de marco/SS; 109 (LO RT), Viktor/AS; 109 (LO LE), duncan1890/GI; 110, LauriPatterson/GI; 111 (Poland), lukszczepanski/AS; 111 (Greece), Netfalls/AS; 111 (Mexico), javarman/AS; 111 (LO), kajakiki/GI; 112 (UP RT), sikarin supphatada/SS; 112 (LO LE), Nikole Mock/EyeEm/GI; 112 (LO RT), vainillaychile/GI; 113 (UP), Studio Gi/AS; 113 (CTR), Jaroslav Moravcik/Dreamstime; 113 (LO), grey/AS; 114, virtustudio/AS; 115 (UP), StockImageFactory/AS; 115 (LO), jsp/SS; 116, CHRISsadowski/GI; 117 (UP), Tom Curtis/SS; 117 (LO), M. Unal Ozmen/SS; 118, Owen Franken/GI; 119 (UP), Nilsz/Dreamstime; 119 (LO), Dmitry Pichugin/SS; 119 (pepper), Tiger Images/SS; 120, ShutterWorx/GI; 121 (CTR), Jiang Hongyan/SS; 121 (RT), Westend61/GI; 122 (LE), natalia9/AS; 122 (RT), Richard Griffin/AS; 123, vkuslandia/AS; 124, Philip Lange/SS; 125 (UP), Jackson Pearson/AS; 125 (CTR), MaraZe/SS; 126, somegirl/AS; 127 (UP), diane555/GI; 127 (LO), baibaz/SS; **Chapter 6:** 128 (UP LE), svetamart/AS; 128 (UP RT), yukihipo/AS; 128 (LO LE), Richard Thornton/SS; 129 (LE), Tetra Images/GI; 129 (UP RT), Elena Schweitzer/AS; 129 (LO RT), Sorin Rechitan/EyeEm/GI; 130 (UP), Steve Allen/SS; 130 (LO), Eric Isselee/SS; 131, Smit/SS; 132, effective stock photos/SS; 132 (wreath), Preechath/AS; 133 (UP CTR), Svitlana-ua/SS; 133 (UP RT), Eric Isselée/AS; 133 (LO), Susan Flashman/SS; 134, Elena Schweitzer/AS; 135 (CTR), Michael Nicholson/Corbis via GI; 135 (LO), Luis Louro/AS; 136 (LE), Riderfoot/Dreamstime; 136 (RT), MAOYAN/SS; 137 (UP), fotogestoeber/AS; 137 (RT), Roman Shisterov/Dreamstime; 137 (LO), KSIVA/SS; 138, FotoFealing/GI; 139 (UP), Robert Eastman/SS; 139 (LO), AP Photo/Gene J. Puskar; 140, Look and Learn/BI; 141, Jason Langley/AL; 142, Eriko Koga/GI; 142 (inset), lily/AS; 143 (UP), Alisa/AS; 143 (LO), Dmitriy Krasko/SS; 144 (UP), JackF/AS; 144 (LO LE), JoffreyM/SS; 144 (LO RT), Lolostock/SS; 145 (UP), Maksim Shebeko/AS; 145 (RT), Mahyuddin Mustafa/SS; 145 (LO), Hue Ta/SS; 146, inomasa/GI; 147 (rat), Jagodka/SS; 147 (ox), Eric Isselee/SS; 147 (cat), Alena Ozerova/AS; 148, Ivy Close Images/AL; 149 (UP), Vera Kuttelvaserova/AS; 149 (LO), AdelevSchalkwyk/GI; 150, Christine/AS; 151, Tetra Images/GI; **Chapter 7:** 152 (UP), olga pink/AS; 152 (LO LE), Microgen/AS; 152 (LO RT), Image Source/GI; 153 (LE), mountainpix/SS; 153 (RT), Michael Betts/GI; 154, URAIWONS/SS; 155 (UP), Eric Isselée/AS; 155 (LO), Per Magnus Persson/GI; 156, Bruce Bisping/Star Tribune via GI; 157, Susan Sheldon/Dreamstime; 157 (dog), Willee Cole/AS; 158, Irina/AS; 158 (hat), Magdalena/AS; 159, andersphoto/SS; 160 (UP RT), Everett Collection, Inc.; 160 (LO RT), Apic/GI; 160 (LO LE), Universal History Archive/UIG via GI; 161 (LE), mrk movie/AL; 161 (UP RT), Courtesy Everett Collection; 161 (LO RT), Courtesy Everett Collection; 162, samott/AS; 163 (LE), Look and Learn/BI; 163 (RT), Gerard Julien/AFP via GI; 165 (LE), 4x6/GI; 165 (RT), Look and Learn/BI; 166, Taweesak Jaroensin/SS; 166 (UP), Grant Dixon/GI; 167 (UP LE), Daniel Thornberg/AS; 167 (UP RT), Richard Philp, London/BI; 167 (LO), Stephanie Deal/GI; 168 (UP), ZU_09/GI; 168 (CTR), Ilja Generalov/SS; 168 (LO LE), Fred Hirschmann/RGB Ventures/SuperStock/AL; 168 (LO CTR), Pictures from History/BI; 169 (UP), Universal History Archive/GI; 169 (LO LE), Nicholas Piccillo/SS; 169 (LO RT), AP Photo; 170, B2M Productions/GI; 171 (UP LE), Ryan McVay/GI; 171 (UP RT), Jaroslav Moravcik/Dreamstime; 171 (LO), art info/BI; 172-173 (CTR), Yong Hian Lim/AS; 172 (giraffe), AS; 172 (LO), Songquan Deng/SS; 173 (giraffe), prapass/SS;

173 (RT), Geo. P. Hall & Son/The New York Historical Society/GI; 174, Stefan Schurr/AS; 175 (UP), The Stapleton Collection/BI; 175 (LO), Rasulov/AS; **Chapter 8:** 176 (UP), Sand Timer/GI; 176 (LO LE), yogo/SS; 176 (LO CTR), Irochka/Dreamstime; 177 (UP), Christie's Images/BI; 177 (CTR), Jose Fuste Raga/GI; 177 (LO), Tero Hakala/SS; 178, Celiafoto/SS; 179, GrashAlex/SS; 180, API/Gamma-Rapho via GI; 181 (UP), Image Source; 181 (reeds), noppharat/AS; 181 (man), Andrew Norouzian/SS; 182, Viacheslav Lopatin/SS; 183 (UP), chomplearn_2001/AS; 183 (LO), Ristic Sacha/SS; 184 (LE), jallfree/GI; 184 (RT), Marko Stamatovic/AS; 185 (UP LE), NAVAPON/AS; 185 (UP RT), Kris Davidson/GI; 185 (LO LE), J. Palys/SS; 185 (LO RT), Alison Wright/GI; 186-187, Leigh Prather/SS; 186 (LE), Culture Club/GI; 187 (CTR), BI; 187 (LO), chekilino85/SS; 188 (LE), Sergey Yarochkin/AS; 188 (RT), evannovostro/AS; 189, North Wind Picture Archives/AL; 190, 3drenderings/SS; 191 (LE), alanmc67/AS; 191 (RT), Prisma Archivo/AL; 192 (LE), BI; 192 (RT), Sabena Jane Blackbird/AL; 193 (LE), BI; 193 (RT), G. Dagli Orti/De Agostini Picture Library/BI; 194, Warchi/GI; 195 (LE), OlekStock/AS; 195 (fire), Ilya Akinshin/SS; 195 (RT), DeAgostini/GI; 196 (LE), Fxquadro/AS; 196 (RT), Grzegorz Michalowski/PAP Photos/Photoshot/Newscom; 197, Christie's Images/BI; 198, aluxum/GI; 199 (UP), Look and Learn/BI; 199 (LO), B Christopher/AL; **Chapter 9:** 200 (UP), elroce/AS; 200 (LO), stocknroll/GI; 201 (LE), BaLL LunLa/SS; 201 (UP RT), Tetra Images/GI; 201 (LO RT), Photographee.eu/AS; 202, chandlerphoto/GI; 203 (UP), Iurii Kalinin/SS; 203 (LO), Fine Art Images/Heritage Images/GI; 204 (LE), cynoclub/AS; 204 (RT), Milosz_G/SS; 205, BI; 206, joecicak/GI; 207, Cultura Creative/AL; 208, stockstudioX/GI; 209 (UP LE), ralucacohn/AS; 209 (UP RT), Mile Atanasov/SS; 209 (CTR LE), tapong117/AS; 209 (LO RT), Bilanol/SS; 210, David Aguilar/ESA/NASA/SOHO; 211 (UP), ArenaCreative/AS; 211 (LO), Yoshikazu Tsuno/AFP via GI; 212 (UP), Soulartist/SS; 212 (animals), adogslifephoto/AS; 212 (CTR), Krafla/AS; 212 (LO), Studio Light and Shade/SS; 213, Dmitri Ma/SS; 214-215, dcw25/AS; 214 (dog), vivienstock/AS; 215 (LO), DeAgostini/GI); 216, jagodka/AS; 217 (UP), MediaProduction/GI; 217 (LO), mlorenzphotography/GI; 218 (UP), Wailam Hui/EyeEm/GI; 218 (CTR), MediaProduction/GI; 219, Lightspring/SS; 220 (background), DNY59/GI; 220 (LE), viktoriya89/AS; 220 (RT), Eric Isselee/SS; 221 (LE), BI; 221 (RT), htoto911/AS; 222-223, goir/AS; 223 (inset), ksena32/AS; 223 (UP), Wisanu Boonrawd/SS; 223 (LO), Pictorial Parade/Archive Photos/GI/GI; **Chapter 10:** 224 (UP LE), Prostock-studio/AS; 224 (UP RT), Javier brosch/AS; 224 (LO LE), Cammy Mountifield/EyeEm/GI; 225 (UP), gupi/AS; 225 (CTR), Primastock/AS; 225 (LO), Idambeer/Dreamstime; 226, zhu difeng/AS; 226 (bulldog), demidoff/AS; 226 (beagle), Eric Isselée/AS; 226 (LO), sosiukin/AS; 227 (UP), Gary Leonard/Corbis via GI; 227 (CTR), BI; 227 (LO), Dimijana/SS; 228 (UP), sunabesyou/AS; 228 (LO), Maria_Janus/SS; 228-229 (CTR), Eric Buermeyer/SS; 229 (UP), Universal History Archive/Universal Images Group via GI; 230 (CTR), voren1/AS; 230 (LO), Sanjida Rashid; 231 (UP), Science & Society Picture Library/GI; 231 (LO), H_Ko/AS; 232 (UP), batya/AS; 232 (bear), Vishnevskiy Vasily/SS; 232 (CTR), Kokhanchikov/AS; 232 (LO), Michael Kraus/SS; 233 (UP LE), michaklootwijk/AS; 233 (RT), aneduard/AS; 233 (LO), mokee81/AS; 234 (UP), Winston Link/SS; 234 (LO), Arsgera/SS; 235, abramsdesign/AS; 236, piyaphunjun/AS; 237 (background), Ilya Akinshin/SS; 237 (UP), topseller/SS; 237 (CTR), mikeledray/SS; 238, yoki5270/AS; 239 (UP), Don Troiani/BI; 239 (LO), ifong/SS; 240 (UP), Marina/AS; 240 (CTR), Rasulov/AS; 240 (LO), BI; 241 (UP LE), Science & Society Picture Library/GI; 241 (UP RT), Grigorita Ko/AS; 241 (LO), FoxPictures/SS; 242 (LE), Vancouver Maritime Museum/BI; 242 (RT), Library of Congress Prints and Photographs Division; 243 (LE), Chris Hill/SS; 243 (inset), Marilyn Gould/Dreamstime; 243 (RT), A. Dagli Orti/De Agostini Picture Library/BI; 244, gertrudda/AS; 245 (LE), FotoAndalucia/AS; 245 (inset), vitaliiy_73/AS; 245 (RT), DUANGJAN J/SS; 246, Krakenimages/SS; 247 (UP), De Agostini/Biblioteca/GI; 247 (LO LE), Oscar White/Corbis/VCG via GI; 247 (LO RT), Rasulov/AS; **Back matter:** 255, Irina/AS; 255 (hat), Magdalena/AS

For Grandma, who's full of surprising stories —**SWD**

Since 1888, the National Geographic Society has funded more than 12,000 research, exploration, and preservation projects around the world. The Society receives funds from National Geographic Partners, LLC, funded in part by your purchase. A portion of the proceeds from this book supports this vital work. To learn more, visit natgeo.com/info.

NATIONAL GEOGRAPHIC and Yellow Border Design are trademarks of the National Geographic Society, used under license.

For more information, visit nationalgeographic.com, call 1-877-873-6846, or write to the following address:

National Geographic Partners
1145 17th Street N.W.
Washington, D.C. 20036-4688 U.S.A.

Visit us online at nationalgeographic.com/books

For librarians and teachers: nationalgeographic.com/books/librarians-and-educators/

More for kids from National Geographic: natgeokids.com

National Geographic Kids magazine inspires children to explore their world with fun yet educational articles on animals, science, nature, and more. Using fresh storytelling and amazing photography, *Nat Geo Kids* shows kids ages 6 to 14 the fascinating truth about the world—and why they should care. **kids.nationalgeographic.com/subscribe**

For rights or permissions inquiries, please contact National Geographic Books Subsidiary Rights: bookrights@natgeo.com

Designed by Ashita.Design

The publisher would like to thank everyone who made this book possible: Ariane Szu-Tu, editor; Catherine Frank, project editor; Sanjida Rashid, art director; Sarah J. Mock, senior photo editor; Hillary Leo, photo editor; Alix Inchausti, production editor; Gus Tello and Anne LeongSon, design production assistants; Jennifer Geddes, fact-checker; and Paula Lee, sensitivity reviewer.

Trade paperback ISBN: 978-1-4263-3865-6
Reinforced library binding ISBN: 978-1-4263-3866-3

Printed in Hong Kong
20/PPHK/1

AAAND ... CUT!

DIRECTOR

NERD OUT!

If you like to learn about how things came to be, you're sure to love *Nerd A to Z*. It's packed with must-know facts from history, science, music, pop culture, and more. Cool photos, quizzes, and quotes from Nerds of Note add to the fun.

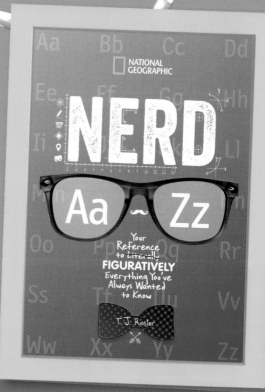